RABBIT HOLE

JON RICHTER

This book is for my siblings: Sam, Amy, Faye and Natalie. I could not live without the help, support and thoughtfulness of these four amazing humans.

'But I don't want to go among mad people,' Alice remarked.
'Oh, you can't help that,' said the Cat: 'we're all mad here.'
– Lewis Carroll, Alice's Adventures in Wonderland

1

PODCAST EPISODE 1:

THE GIRL

Hi there, true crime fans. I'm Elaine Napier, and you're listening to *The Frozen Files*, the new podcast where we reopen ice-cold cases in search of the truth for people that justice has forgotten. For this, our first series, we'll be focusing on the fascinating and tragic story of Katrin Gunnarsdottir.

Katrin disappeared five years ago after taking a late-night taxi home from Gatwick airport. It was a cold January evening in 2013, and she had just been to her native Iceland to visit her parents following the death of her grandmother. The twenty-five-year-old's flight home was delayed by six hours, so by the time she arrived, she had missed the last train back into London.

Her breath misted in the frosty air, her blonde hair tucked away under her hood as she stood outside the airport, glad of the thick coat she had taken for the trip to Reykjavik. Stars gleamed brightly above as she called her boyfriend to ask for a lift, but his car was in the garage with a broken exhaust, so he suggested she order a Ryde to her apartment instead.

Here's what else we know.

We know she took his advice, ordered a taxi, and was picked up at exactly twenty minutes past midnight.

We know that her boyfriend, Marcus Dobson, claims he did not hear from her following the phone call. When she did not return his messages or arrive at his apartment the following evening as arranged, he started to contact her friends and work colleagues, and eventually called the police to report her missing.

We know from Ryde's records that the driver, who we'll call John H, arrived at Katrin's home in Elephant and Castle at 0137, and that her suitcase was found inside the apartment by police; but there was no sign that she had slept in the bed, made any food, or spent any time there. We also know that Katrin did not arrive at work the next day and, apparently, did not contact anyone else after her call with Marcus. She was never seen alive again.

What we don't know – what neither the police, nor the private investigator hired by her family, nor any of the online sleuths that have picked and probed at Katrin's case over the subsequent years, have been able to ascertain – is what happened to her.

But someone must know. Because beautiful young women don't just vanish into the winter mist. The awful truth is that when they disappear, it's because they have been abducted, drugged, raped, sold to human trafficking gangs, murdered.

I know that Katrin's parents have been destroying themselves with such speculation for years, and I don't want them to suffer the hellish uncertainty of a missing daughter any longer. And neither do I want the person, or people, responsible for her disappearance to escape justice.

So I've made it my business to solve the mystery.

I'll be providing weekly updates on my investigation, so please subscribe to the podcast to hear the latest news. And please, please let us know your thoughts on Twitter, or get in touch via our Facebook discussion forum, because if there's one thing I can bring to this puzzle that the police don't have access to, it's *you*: your thoughts, your insights, your ideas, your suggestions.

Together, I firmly believe we can crack this case.

2

'One.'

Napier grimaced in determination and flung her fist at the pad.

'One, two.'

Another left jab, with as much snap as she could muster, followed by a sluggish right cross.

'One, two, three.'

Jab, cross, left hook. Her punches were growing increasingly weak and ineffectual. But she kept going: after all, soon she would have to survive three whole rounds of this punishment.

'One, two, three, four.' The buzzer sounded, muffling Martina's final syllable, but Napier knew her coach would still expect her to complete the set. She clenched her jaw once again, picturing the pads replaced by the pair of faces she'd most like to cave in; the only trouble was that there were many more than two. She settled for Sycophantic Steve at the *Chron*, and Tim, her most recent (but by no means most detestable) ex, and slammed her gloves into the pads once again, snarling with venom as she drove the uppercut into what she imagined to be

Steve's chin. Then she sagged to the floor, breathless, her body dripping with sweat.

'Now give me twenty push-ups,' came her coach's unforgiving baritone. Napier looked up pleadingly, but the expression on the Italian's face was pitiless.

It's all right for you, Napier thought as she struggled into position. *You're still in your twenties and have a body like a bunch of elevator cables.* 'Do you delight in torturing people?' she hissed as she lowered herself to the boxing ring's sweat-stained canvas.

'First push-ups, then talk.'

Napier's eyes narrowed as she forced herself upwards. *You try doing this when you're pushing forty and drink too much.* Push-ups while wearing boxing gloves were hard. All the pressure had to be exerted through her balled fists instead of open palms, and she gasped with the effort as she dropped her nose to the mat, then forced herself back up into a plank position.

'Keep your core engaged,' Martina barked, and Napier fantasised for a moment about 'accidentally' landing one of the left jabs right on her coach's pretty face during their next session. Not that she was insane enough to try it; when she wasn't working as a personal trainer and boxing instructor, Martina Mazziotto was a semi-professional MMA fighter with a 4-0 win record.

Fourteen.

The Italian might be small, but Napier knew she was training with an extremely tough woman.

Fifteen.

But then Napier knew she was tough too; in different ways perhaps, ways that made her a tenacious journalist.

Sixteen.

Ways that some of her male colleagues had struggled to deal with.

Seventeen.

Ways that had driven those colleagues to engineer her exit from the *East London Chronicle*, where she'd worked for fifteen years.

Eighteen.

Well, good riddance to those tossers. She was happier now than she'd been for a long time. And the podcast was going to be a roaring success.

Nineteen.

Either that, or she would die–

Twenty.

–trying. Her arms buckled and she crumpled to the floor, panting like an exhausted animal.

'Okay,' came Martina's voice from above her. 'The session is finished. You did pretty good.' Napier wondered if this was a deliberate coaching strategy: dispensing compliments so rarely that they felt hard-won and treasured when they came. 'Maybe you will not get completely killed in this fight.'

Or perhaps she's just brutally honest.

'Thanks,' Napier replied sarcastically, hauling herself into a sitting position. 'Can I ask you...' She paused, trying to catch her breath. 'How many sessions you did with Katrin?'

Martina frowned. 'I thought we agree not to talk about the dead girl.'

The dead girl. So many people made that assumption. Herself included, at times.

'I just want to know what sort of student she was.'

She could see how uncomfortable the fighter had become. It was hard to understand: this was a woman who Napier had seen in a video fighting inside a cage, blood gushing from her smashed nose and mangled lips, looking completely at ease as she battled a ruthless opponent inside the terrifying structure. Yet Martina visibly squirmed whenever Napier mentioned her investigation into the disappearance of her former student.

Investigation?

She glanced around at the brightly-lit, bustling gym, where Katrin had trained with Martina for her 'white-collar' boxing match. Napier had joined the same gym shortly after she'd decided to move close to where Katrin used to live and work.

More like an obsession.

'She was a very happy person,' Martina answered eventually, grasping for the words in a language she did not speak perfectly. 'Maybe too happy. Not enough steel. And always distracted by the men.'

Katrin had lost her fight. Napier had seen that footage, too. She had no idea why such a gorgeous girl, intelligent and popular and with a great career ahead of her, would want to climb into a boxing ring and get smacked in the face for six full minutes.

Just six minutes... it sounds like an eternity, and also like nothing at all.

And yet here she was, training for the exact same event. She didn't quite understand it herself. She certainly wasn't going to mention it on the podcast; she didn't want to make the story all about herself. So then why was she doing the fight at all? At first she'd rationalised it as a perfect opportunity to meet and interview the people Katrin had befriended at the gym, where the missing girl had trained almost every day.

But Napier knew it was more than that. An attempt to better identify with Katrin, maybe, or a misguided sense of dramatic symmetry. Perhaps the preposterous idea that if she won her own fight it would grant Katrin's belated absolution.

Or maybe something else, something darker.

'Do you mean any specific men?' she asked.

Martina regarded her cautiously, then slowly nodded.

3

PODCAST EPISODE 2:

THE BOYFRIEND

My intention with this podcast is not to express opinions. It is simply to capture and relay facts, and to explore possibilities. Wherever I can I will present evidence in the form of taped interviews, or transcripts if the subject is not happy for me to use their voice.

One of the reasons I want to avoid idle speculation is because it can destroy people. People like Marcus Dobson, Katrin's boyfriend, who was apparently the last person she spoke to. Marcus was never charged with any crime; yet not only has he had to deal with the disappearance of his beloved girlfriend, but also his own subsequent arrest and many hours of questioning. And that's not to mention the unrelenting and brutal social media campaign against him.

Regardless of any opinions on his guilt or innocence, Marcus has undoubtedly suffered; when I met him at his home in Walthamstow, he was the epitome of a broken man. Following his arrest, he lost his job at KPMG, and now works for a small local accounting firm preparing tax returns. The handsome twenty-something I saw in countless photographs with Katrin, tanned and muscular and always smiling, has been replaced by a pale, gaunt thirty-one-year-old, who fidgeted nervously throughout my visit. His hands shook as he placed my cup of tea on the coffee table, their fingernails chewed painfully raw.

Marcus was kind enough to allow me to record our interview.

'Can you tell me about her?'

'She was beautiful. I know that's such a trite thing to say. Everyone says that about their girlfriends or their wives or their daughters; it's what Hollywood has taught us to say, you know? But in this case it was completely true. She was beautiful, on the outside, on the inside, everywhere. Just a wonderful person.'

'That's very sweet. How did the two of you first meet?'

'We went to uni together, in Nottingham. We both did economics. My work was probably atrocious for those first few weeks, while all I did was moon over her. It took me a month to realise that I had to either ask her out or quit the course.'

'And you were together for six years?'

'That's right. I thought it would last forever. But I was wrong; I guess it was unrealistic to think the world would let me keep her. I knew I didn't deserve her, but I thought that, somehow, my luck would just never run out. After all, someone has to win the lottery, right?'

He flashed a sad smile at me at this point, and I saw a hint of the boyish charm that must have first enchanted Katrin, all those years ago.

'Can you tell me what happened that night?'

Marcus spilled his tea at this point, so the recording broke off while he apologised profusely and mopped it up. He didn't do a particularly thorough job, and I noticed the apartment's general state of uncleanliness and disrepair. 'Squalid' would be an unfair description, but the small, filthy flat wasn't too far away. Eventually we resumed, although the tiny accident seemed to have completely shot Marcus's nerves. He gnawed mercilessly at his fingers as he talked, to the point where I thought he would draw blood.

'She called me. I knew her flight had been delayed, but I'd already told her my car was in the garage until Monday, so I wouldn't be able to pick her up. I thought she just wanted to let me know she'd landed safely, but I think she expected me still to be able to somehow come and collect her. I told her it made no sense for me to get a taxi all the way there and back when she could just get one straight here.'

'Here?'

'I was trying to persuade her to come round. I wanted to see her.'

'But she went straight home instead?'

'Yes. Maybe she was angry with me because of the car. But it had needed that repair for weeks.'

'Do you still have the car?'

'No. I scrapped it when the police eventually gave it back.'

Of course. Along with their questioning, the police ran tests on Marcus's car; they'd wanted to check whether he'd used it to dispose of her body. They'd also repeatedly searched the apartment he was then renting in Notting Hill. They even dug up the lawn at the rear of the building in case he had buried her there; this despite the garden being in full view of a number of overlooking flats, and no one having witnessed or reported anything.

'So she agreed to get a Ryde?'

'That's right.'

The driver was also thoroughly investigated. John H, who was forty-eight at the time of Katrin's disappearance, and had been working for Ryde for almost a year, claims he unloaded Katrin's suitcase for her, but that she declined his offer of help to carry it inside. He watched her drag the case into the apartment building, then tinkered with his phone for a few minutes while he located his next customer.

Ryde's tracking records prove that John H did indeed stop at her address for six minutes before moving again. Given that the car hadn't stopped since collecting her at the airport, the driver would have had to subdue Katrin, steal her keys, take her suitcase up to her apartment, then hide her body somewhere, all within that six-minute window. The police had tested this and deemed it an impossible feat. Add to that the fact that no evidence was found either in her apartment or in the taxi, and the testimony of John H's next passenger who confirmed they had been picked up at 0152 and remembered nothing suspicious about his behaviour, and it seems clear that John was not involved.

'Do you think the taxi driver is innocent?'

'Yes. Because the man in the white van did it. Even if no one else believes he exists.'

'The Coughing Man?'

'I never called him that.'

'I'm sorry. That's the label he's been given on the internet. There are plenty of online sleuths who believe you, Marcus.'

'Then why can nobody find him?'

His eyes seemed suddenly pleading, wide and sad and strained with desperation. What I said next sounds a little like cheap self-promotion, and I hope you will forgive me; I didn't mean to sound crass, I just genuinely believe that I – we – can help him.

'That's what this podcast is about, Marcus. If we get more people talking about the specifics of the case, more people who might remember something... if we can stir up even a fragment of a new lead, then it will have been worthwhile.'

'Yes. I hope so.'

'Can you tell me about him? The Coughing Man?'

Marcus's expression darkened then, and for the first time I saw a different side of this bereaved man, a shadow of immense bitterness and anger. 'She said he sat next to her on the flight. They checked the manifest, and that seat was supposed to be empty.'

'Can you describe him?'

'She didn't go into detail. She just said she'd been sat next to some annoying creep on the plane, that he'd been really repulsive: overweight and smelly, with shabby clothes and a huge scruffy beard. He kept coughing and sneezing like he had the flu, and she hoped she hadn't caught it.'

'Was he young or old?'

'I don't remember. Maybe she didn't say. I've spent so long racking my brains over the years, trying to remember every single word of that call, in case there's something significant I've missed. I remember she said his beard looked like it probably had old fragments of food stuck in it, like Mr Twit from the Roald Dahl book.'

'And he offered to drive her home?'

'Yes. She said he insisted on talking to her, even when she put her headphones in. Kept offering her a lift home in his van. She only mentioned him at all because she saw a white van idling nearby while she was talking to me, and thought maybe it was him, watching her. She said the van was just like him, all grimy and disgusting.'

'Did she see the driver?'

'No. I asked her, but it was too dark. She said the van was all rusted, and had a weird logo on the side, like the sign of the evil eye.'

I can't help but get goosebumps as I listen to his words. The symbol is supposed to ward off evil, but in this context it sounds horribly sinister. Perhaps *too* sinister; remember that we only have Marcus's word that the call took place at all. The white van, its ominous emblem, and the mysterious Coughing Man could all be sheer fabrications.

'There's every chance it could have been someone else's vehicle.'

'It was him.' Marcus seemed absolutely convinced, and I found it hard to sustain my doubts. It seemed that this was what he'd been clinging to for all these years, the one lead that gave him the smallest shred of hope of finding the truth. 'I think he followed the taxi, and then followed her into her building.'

'Wouldn't the Ryde driver have seen something?'

'Not if he was faffing about with his phone, or if the van driver waited until he'd moved on.'

'But no one else from the flight remembers this man, and no one has been able to locate the van either. Although there must be thousands of white vans in London.'

'Not one with an eye painted on the side. Believe me, I've been searching. Sometimes I go out at night and just drive around the streets, looking for that fucking bastard. Every time I see a white van I get a little knot of adrenaline in my throat, and I start shaking, and feeling like I'm going to be sick. I look at the driver and think *Maybe it's you*. But it isn't, because I'll know. When I find him, I'll know.'

I looked at the intensity in his face, and shuddered. The fruitless quest seemed to have aged him horribly, to have wasted the flesh from his bones and toxified his mind.

I finished my tea and left soon after that, reflecting on the damage that obsession can do.

4

'It sounds really good, Isaac,' said Napier, removing her headphones and smiling across the table at him. 'I'm not sure if I like the ending music, though.'

Her friend looked mildly put out. 'It's just a placeholder, some free shite I found on the internet. We can easily change it.'

'Can I have "Red Right Hand"?'

'Not unless you phone up Nick Cave and ask his permission. That's why everyone uses the free shite. The problem is that you hear the same free ones all the time; in all honesty, I've heard that song on about ten different podcasts already. I even used it in a video game I made once: a Lovecraftian horror sports simulator called *Cthulympics*. It... didn't sell very well.'

He looked momentarily downcast, but she just smiled again. It was good to see him. Isaac Jones never changed: tall but stooped, long-limbed but graceless, bald but handsome in a quirky, Billy Corgan sort of way. Serious in a manner that always made her laugh. She agreed with the summary on his grubby T-shirt, which proudly affirmed him as a 'Nerd Before It Was Cool'.

They were sitting in a coffee shop close to Meadowvale's

tube station. As well as his laptop and their drinks – his, something chilled and an alarming bright green colour, hers a strong black Americano – the table was covered with the mess of notes she had been working on before he arrived, the remnants of her croissant scattered around them like flakes of dead skin. She'd expected to be scolded for still not having made the switch to a computer, but Isaac had been working with her for so long that he seemed to have given up lecturing her. They had met at the *Chronicle*, where he'd worked in the IT department until he left years before she did. He was now making most of his money trading cryptocurrencies.

'Do you think the length is okay?' she asked. 'I didn't want to go into too much detail in the first one, but I'm hoping the episodes will be longer once they get going.'

He shrugged. 'I suppose if there's enough interesting material, it doesn't matter how long they are. How many episodes do you think the series will run?'

She knew that other people, friends and colleagues, thought there was something between them; there wasn't, though, and never had been. Their friendship had always seemed so effortless, refreshingly detached from the baggage of other people's expectations. Even as they both approached their forties, resolutely single, there wasn't even the merest suggestion that they ought to 'give it a go'; and besides, Isaac was far too misanthropic to date *anybody*. Whenever their conversation turned towards relationships, Isaac would inevitably be the one listening patiently to the story of her latest car crash, his withering expression making her misadventures seem trivial and tragically comic. She supposed he was like the brother she never had.

(One day she'd get around to telling him about her sister. For now, though, it suited her to let him believe she was another only child, like him.)

'Depends what I find out. I think I've got enough to cover the first four or five. I even managed to get a taped interview with her parents this week.'

'I bet that was depressing.'

'Yup. But I did find out they once hired a private investigator, so if I manage to track him down that could yield a ton of extra material.'

'Is he still working on the case?'

'No. They parted ways a few years ago, after he couldn't solve the mystery. He's retired now.'

'What about the Facebook group?' Isaac asked, taking a noisy slurp of his revolting-looking drink. 'Have you had much interest on it?'

'Nothing really. A few people commenting on the first show, saying it sounds interesting and wishing me good luck. I suppose that will change after the first full episode is broadcast and we hit the big time.'

'That's the spirit. Then you can start paying me.'

'Come on, Isaac – you know that as soon as I'm making money I'll be able to afford proper tech support; I won't have to scrape the barrel with the likes of you.'

His raised eyebrow somehow managed to convey the same sentiment as a middle finger. She didn't need to tell him she was joking, of course; he knew how much she appreciated his help. If she was honest, the redundancy had knocked her confidence quite a bit, and this project was the most energised she'd been for months.

'So what are you up to this afternoon?' he asked, glancing around the coffee shop's sanitised interior. Part of a national chain, its recent opening was evidence of the spreading central London 'regeneration effect', whose tendrils were snaking outwards even as far as sleepy Zone 3 enclaves like Meadowvale. It was a Sunday, and the place was getting slowly busier as noon approached. Napier looked around at the other customers, themselves a microcosm of the area's gentrification: people taking a breather while out doing their shopping, labourers on their lunch break, mothers (still always mothers) pushing prams whose occupants stared around, wide eyes greedily sucking in new data. Entrepreneurial types hammering at the keys of their MacBooks. Long-time residents (black) mixing with trendy hipsters that had recently moved there (white).

She wondered if any of them had known Katrin. The missing woman had herself been an agent of the area's transformation, of course.

'I'm going to visit Hannibal Heights.'

'What's that?'

'Katrin was a property developer, before she disappeared. She worked on a big residential tower right here in Meadowvale. The locals call it "The Animal House".'

'Why?'

'You'll have to wait for the episode.' She winked at him, and laughed as his eyebrow was hoisted once again.

5

PODCAST EPISODE 3:

THE TOWER

I'm on my way to Hannibal Heights. Sorry about the noise; that's the rain, which is drenching me while I'm recording this on my dictaphone. It's October, and the weather is unforgivingly British: cold and wet, the sky a cloudy grey soup the colour of gruel.

I'm also sorry if I sound a little breathless. Hannibal Heights is at the top of a hill, and the climb is longer and steeper than it looks; but I wanted to give you a sense of the isolation of the place. Behind me I can still see the town centre, the Underground station, the shops, the people going about their weekend routines. Yet my ascent seems still and quiet, peaceful in an ominous sort of way. Tall, bent trees line the main street, their autumn leaves the colour of rusted machinery. Some cling stubbornly to the branches, while others are heaped on the pavement in sludgy wet piles.

I see the tower at the top of the rise. Katrin worked in property development, and Hannibal Heights was her first big project: it's a residential apartment building with almost 300 flats, forty-three of which are affordable units, which means they belong to an affordable housing trust that charges reduced rents to people on lower incomes. There was a lot of controversy when it was constructed, partly because locals felt there should have been a larger number of affordable homes, and partly because a treasured local museum was demolished to make way for it. I don't want to get into the politics of the country's housing crisis right now, so I'm going to focus on the second point, because that explains why the tower is known in Meadowvale as 'The Animal House'.

Hannibal House was a stately home belonging to Edwin Hannibal, who had inherited it from his father William, along with the vast riches of the family's successful tea-trading business. This wealth afforded Edwin the time and resources to pursue a most unusual hobby, and in 1891 he opened the family home to the public, who were intrigued to find brightly-coloured birds, tropical fish, elk, zebras, tigers and even a polar bear occupying the halls of the Hannibal estate.

But these exotic creatures, which many of London's residents had never seen before in their lives, posed no threat to the visitors – because Edwin was a taxidermist. More accurately, he was a taxidermy enthusiast, as he never personally involved himself in the process of skinning dead animals, treating the hides with preserving chemicals and arranging them on wooden mounts. What he *did* do was spend a fortune travelling overseas to amass the largest collection of its kind in the whole of London. If a species of animal could be named, Edwin Hannibal wanted it stuffed and showcased in his museum. One of the rooms in his exhibition was even dedicated to 'anthropomorphic taxidermy', where animals were portrayed in human-like poses; a classroom full of dead rabbits, or monkeys sitting down to a tea party might sound grotesque to our modern ears, but Victorian audiences found this a charming bit of whimsy.

The institution became known as 'The Animal House', and

continued to display its taxidermy as part of a broader art collection throughout the twentieth century, even when it transferred to public ownership after Edwin's grandson managed to squander what remained of the family's fortune on the more traditional pastime of booze and hard drugs. But as the bizarre attraction became less and less popular, the council decided it could no longer afford to pay for the building's upkeep, and the land was eventually sold to Triton Homes. The museum was demolished to make way for an apartment building, which now looms above me, sleek and modern and angular, like something transported here from the future.

The new tower block was named Hannibal Heights in a nod to the area's history, and the taxidermy collection preserved in a ground floor museum as part of the land deal. Not yet content to stop their homage there, the development team decided to install a huge copper fountain outside the main entrance, depicting a group of animals gathered around a central basin. I'm approaching that fountain now, listening to the weak trickles of water that emerge from the mouths of a lion, a bull, a bear, an eagle, a dolphin, a snake. A layer of greenish oxide covers all of them, and I can't help thinking of mould and decay; the water in the basin is dirty and viscous, the glint of the coins tossed into it barely penetrating the murk.

Whether I like the design of the fountain or not, Katrin Gunnarsdottir was a member of that development team; the building and its creepy water feature are in many ways her lasting legacy. A strange coincidence then, that I am here to meet with someone to enquire about her disappearance. But perhaps not so strange; this building is very popular with young renters, and exactly the sort of place you might live if you were a handsome personal trainer working at the local gym, socialising in the nearby bars and occasionally dating some of your clients.

Which leads me to Jamal Habib, who has just escorted me up to his rented apartment. The building is pleasant enough inside, with carpets and walls an inoffensive shade of grey, a slight shabbiness just starting to set in. I try to imagine the corridors full of motionless monsters, crocodiles and bears and tigers with ferocious snarls frozen into place, but the bland interior seems to deny the site's former denizens.

The décor in Jamal's flat is a little more interesting, his cream-coloured couch and a bright blue lava lamp catching my eye as I follow him inside. He does not occupy one of the affordable units, evidently making a decent living from his coaching job, and has spent a lot of money fitting out his 'lad pad' with an array of luxuries including a TV set the size of an entire wall.

He was kind enough to allow me to play the recording of our interview.

'So, Jamal, tell us about yourself.'

'Er, well, my name's Jamal, and – sorry, you already know that.'

His smile is infectious and I warmed to him immediately. We were sitting at his kitchen table, and he seemed very friendly and happy to talk. He'd already offered me something from his impressive drinks cabinet which, as it wasn't even 4pm yet, I'd politely declined.

'I'm twenty-eight, I'm a PT and I work at SmashFit. I've seen you in there recently, haven't I? Training with Martina?'

'That's right; I'm very much a work in progress. So have you always lived in London?'

'My family moved here from Lebanon when I was three, so yeah, pretty much.'

'Always in Meadowvale?'

'Nope.'

'So your mum and dad live somewhere else?'

'My dad's up in Golders Green. My mum's dead.'

His smile had disappeared, and I noticed how piercing his eyes were. He had an unsettling way of maintaining eye contact while seeming not to blink. He waved away my apology and the smile reappeared again, as if he could switch it on and off at will.

'No worries.'

'You have a very nice apartment.'

'Yeah, I've done all right for myself, innit.'

He seemed uncertain around me, unsure whether to be flirtatious or to treat me with deference.

'Isn't it a bit early for Halloween?'

There were several pumpkins lined up along the windowsill, all different shapes and sizes, some bright orange and others with a green tint that reminded me of the mouldering fountain. His smile widened at my comment and he hopped to his feet, lean and energetic, retrieving one of the gourds and setting it down on the table, facing me. I could see that it was carved into a pretty accurate representation of Jack Skellington from Tim Burton's *The Nightmare Before Christmas*.

'That's my best one, I reckon.'

'Have you always been artistic?'

'I suppose so. I was good at it at school. But you just grow out of it, don't you, I suppose?'

There was something sad and wistful in his voice as he said it, making him seem suddenly much older than his years. We continued chatting like that for a little while, but he knew I was there to talk to him about Katrin, and didn't seem to mind when I turned the conversation towards her.

'How long did you know her for?'

'She trained with me on and off for two years, after she started working nearby.'

'Did you like her?'

'She was a lot of fun. Always laughing, always joking. But she worked hard – she was really determined to lose weight and get lean, not that she needed to.'

'Did you like her in a romantic sense?'

'Well, yeah. Any man would have done.'

'Did anything ever happen between you two?'

'She had a boyfriend.'

'That doesn't answer my question.'

'Who did you even hear this from?'

I'd heard the rumour from one of Jamal's colleagues at the gym, but decided not to reveal my source. Jamal shrugged and didn't push the point, the gesture seeming to suggest he slept with so many women that he might have genuinely forgotten whether he and Katrin were ever involved. But his expression, the sudden sadness in his penetrating eyes, told me that Katrin had been special to him.

Then I asked him when he last saw her, and he dropped a bombshell.

'Right here, at Tony's party.'

'You mean here in Hannibal Heights?'

'Yep. Tony lives a few floors up.'

'Who's Tony?'

'Tony's a promoter. Boxing, MMA, all that stuff. He's in our gym quite a lot.'

'When was the party?'

'It was a Thursday night. The last day of January. I remember because I'd done Dry January that year, but decided to sack it off a bit early. I was wasted after about three cans.'

At the time, I didn't realise. It was only when I was piecing this episode together later that the penny dropped, along with my jaw.

Thursday 31st of January was the night Katrin disappeared.

6

EXTRACT FROM RECORDED INTERVIEW WITH ELAINE NAPIER

Sergeant Rowan: Hi Elaine. I'm Sergeant Rowan. How, um, how are you feeling?

Napier: Hungry.

Rowan: Oh. Well, there's a McDonald's just across the street. I'm sure your mum will take you to get some food very soon. I just need to ask you a few questions first.

Napier: I don't need her to go with me. I'm not a baby.

Rowan: Oh. Sorry. No, of course you're not. Okay, Elaine, I want to talk about your sister. Samantha went missing yesterday, didn't she?

Napier: It's Sam.

Rowan: Sorry; Sam.

Napier: <Inaudible>

Rowan: I know you and your mum must be very worried. We are too. That's why we want to make sure we know exactly what happened. So

I'm going to ask you about what your sister said and did last night.

Napier: She probably just ran away. She did it once before.

Rowan: When was that?

Napier: The last time mum called her a slut.

Rowan: Did your mum call her a slut last night?

Napier: …

Rowan: Please, Elaine. It will help us find out what happened to your sister if you be honest with us.

Napier: I just want to go home.

Rowan: Do you know where your sister went?

Napier: …

Rowan: Where did she go the last time she ran away?

Napier: I think she just went to the park. She came home about three hours later.

Rowan: Is that where she went last night?

Napier: …

Rowan: She told your mum she was going to her friend Emma's.

Napier: Yeah, but that was a lie.

Rowan: What happens at the park?

Napier: I don't know. She says I'm too young to go with her.

Rowan: Do you know if she was meeting anyone there? A boyfriend maybe?

Napier: She has lots of boyfriends.

Rowan: Do they ever come round to your house?

Napier: Nope. My dad won't let them.

Rowan: Oh. <Sound of leafing paper> I thought your dad was—

Napier: So Sam goes to the park to meet them. That's where they all drink beer and get off with each other.

Rowan: Do you know the names of any of her boyfriends?

Napier: <Whispers> It's a secret.

Rowan: Can you tell it to me?

Napier: Sam says she'll punch me if I do.

Rowan: Elaine, please, this is important. If she's run away with a boy she might be in trouble.

Napier: Sam's okay. My dad will look after her.

Rowan: Elaine, your dad isn't… look, no one can protect your sister if we don't know where she is, can they?

Napier: My dad knows where she is. He told Sam he'd always look after us.

Rowan: Elaine, please. If you know the name of who your sister was meeting you need to tell me.

Napier: I can't remember his name. But it's in her diary.

Rowan: She has a diary?

Napier: Yes. It's in her room in her drawer. She locks it but I know where the key is. I read it sometimes. That's where all the names are.

Rowan: And do you think the diary will tell us where she went?

Napier: I told you, Sam went to the park. Can I go home now?

7

'Okay, so this time I fucking *love* the music, Isaac. The tension-building tune at the end sounds ace; I got goosebumps listening to it.'

'I aim to please.'

'Hopefully this episode will get people talking a bit. It's still quiet on the message boards.'

'You need to keep the cliffhangers coming. The interview with her parents might need to wait for another week, maybe?'

'Yeah. I'm going to pay a visit to this Tony character and get his version of events.'

'The fighting promoter? Be careful with yourself, Napes.'

'Hey, I'm a boxer now, remember? I can look after myself.'

He didn't reply. She heard a faint clicking sound down the line.

'You're playing on your PlayStation, aren't you?'

'Mmm? What? Of course not! I'm giving you my undivided– *oh for fuck's sake!*'

She heard what sounded suspiciously like a DualShock controller being hurled across the room.

'Glad you're having a productive evening, Isaac.'

'Look, I'll call you back in ten minutes, I promise.'

'Don't let me distract you from your true love.' She hung up and sagged back into her bed, grimacing at the stabbing pain in her side.

Some boxer.

She was taking six painkillers a day to try to suppress the ache in her ribs, which were at least bruised, if not cracked. The first proper sparring session earlier that week had left her feeling battered, both physically and emotionally.

But the fight was approaching fast, and she couldn't drop out now.

Wincing with the effort, she rolled onto her side and opened her laptop. She had too many windows open, a new tab for each line of enquiry, each idea plunging her deeper into the internet's dark labyrinth. She flicked through them, pausing on Katrin's Facebook page.

The girl's face (Napier thought of her as a girl, which she knew was patronising, but Katrin's features and playful smile were so youthful, seemingly free from all the cares and lines and disappointments and regrets of adulthood) stared back at her, framed by long straw-coloured hair a similar shade to Napier's own. *And to Sam's.* Katrin's wide eyes were the colour of clear blue water, seeming to beckon to Napier through the screen. Eyes you could drown in. Eyes that could enthral, enchant, bewitch.

Napier scrolled down and saw the messages posted on Katrin's wall, friends and family pleading with her to contact them, sending their love, their thoughts, their prayers. Over time the messages dried up, until the last couple of years when only sporadic posts appeared, clustered around the anniversary of Katrin's disappearance, and in December, when a post from her parents read, 'Happy birthday to our little angel'.

Napier felt a pulse of anger course through her. Gritting her teeth, she clicked on the next tab, where she had looked up Tony online, or more accurately Anthony Weaver, the full name Jamal had given her. He was indeed a fighting promoter, organising an array of events including boxing, MMA, Thai boxing, and even bare-knuckle competitions. He also acted as an agent to a handful of professional and semi-professional fighters.

There were two other interesting things about Tony.

The first was that Martina Mazziotto was currently signed with him, and had been since her first fight.

The other was that he was the organiser of the white-collar boxing event that Napier herself had signed up to. The same event Katrin had entered, a few months before her disappearance.

8

PODCAST EPISODE 4:

THE PROMOTER

'Who else was at the party, Jamal?'

'It was pretty busy, to be honest. Tony's flat is huge. There were a ton of people from the gym, from the other boxing club, plus loads of randoms I've never seen before...'

That's me on the phone to Jamal. I called him after I realised the significance of the date of the party, but he couldn't really remember much else about it. Like he'd already told me, he was pretty hammered.

'Did you invite her there?'

'No, no, I was surprised to see her. We spoke for a bit but I was, uhh... I left with someone, you know.'

'Do you know who she was there with?'

'She was with a couple of her friends, who I knew from the gym. Work colleagues, maybe. I can't remember their names though, if that's what you're asking. Sorry.'

Katrin must have arrived home from the airport, dropped off her suitcase, and then decided to travel to Hannibal Heights. A busy party, on a Thursday night, with her friends. Attended by possibly the last people to see her alive.

Maybe even by her killer.

I needed to find out who else had been in attendance. If Jamal couldn't remember, I wondered if the party's host could enlighten me. Which is how I ended up at Meadowvale Community Gardens, in the rain, watching Tony Weaver digging in his allotment.

He is a paradox of a man; exactly what you'd expect from a retired cage fighter, and exactly what you wouldn't. Born and raised in London, he moved to the States to pursue an MMA career, retiring in the mid-noughties with a reasonable win/loss record and a mouth full of silver teeth that had earned him the nickname 'The Dentist'. He is of below average height, but as wide as a wardrobe, with close-cropped hair on top of a head as squat and hard as an artillery shell. His nose has been broken so many times that it resembles a lump of clay mashed into the centre of his face, and the network of scars across his forehead read like an elegy of violence.

And yet, talking to Tony in this tranquil setting, I found him a calm and reflective person, eloquent and businesslike. He was unwilling to let me broadcast our interview, so my sound technician Isaac is attempting his best impersonation of a cockney hardman as he reads the transcript.

'How long have you been a farmer, Tony?'

'You mean a gardener.'

'Well, it looks like you're growing a few vegetables there.'

'It's still called gardening, if you do it on a small scale.'

The twisting tattoos creeping up his neck, clearly visible against his chalk-white skin, looked like something sprouting beneath his collar, as though his plants were beginning to take possession of his body.

'I didn't know you could grow anything in autumn.'

'Well, you can. Onions, garlic, spinach. I've even got a herb garden over there, see.'

'It's very nice.'

'It is. I suppose this is my way of getting away from it all.' He tilted his face towards the rain, which continued to fall in a light drizzle. 'When you've had a life like mine, you appreciate a bit of peace.'

'But you must still enjoy the fighting, right? You're a very successful promoter.'

'A man can only do what he knows. You've got to keep going somehow, haven't you?' He flashed his alarming metallic smile. 'People are like plants, I suppose; some stay tall and strong, others shrivel up and die.'

I nodded as silence descended for a moment, interrupted only by the gently pattering rain, and the distant sound of a train grinding along the track that bisected the Gardens on the other side of the woods. The place felt eerily remote, a haven amidst the chaos of the city. Then I noticed Tony fingering the peculiar necklace he was wearing, and asked him what it was.

'This? Just me teeth, innit. They usually find them and give them back to you when they get knocked out, and after a while I'd amassed quite a collection. So I paid someone to drill holes in 'em and put them on a chain. Does it frighten you?'

I told him that it did, a little. Everything about his world did. 'Did Katrin seem frightened, when she fought her boxing match?'

'Ahh, there it is. The segue.'

'You knew that's who I wanted to talk to you about.'

He returned to his digging, or more accurately to turning the earth over with his spade, planting seeds. 'The honest truth is I don't really remember her. We put on so many of those shows. I don't make much money out of them, mind – most of the proceeds go to charity.'

'But she came to your flat.'

'If you say so.'

'Didn't you invite her?'

'Not my style. You just sort of put the word out and see who turns up. More fun that way.'

'You must be a popular man.'

'Nah, just a sad old party animal. It's not like there's a Mrs Weaver to stop me anymore.'

He grinned. He was referring to his ex-wife. I found out later that they divorced in 2006, with her taking custody of their two daughters, then aged five and three. He has a third daughter with a different woman, from whom he has also since separated.

'Look, Tony, I appreciate you probably can't remember the specifics of a party at your flat five years ago. But please try.' I held out a photograph of Katrin, one I obtained from her parents. In the picture she is smiling her usual mischievous smile, her eyes large and childlike. A face full of enthusiasm, excited about the life she thought she had ahead of her. 'That's her. Can you remember anything at all from that night?'

He drove the spade into the mud with a grunt; not angrily, just a precise and powerful movement, leaving it planted firmly in place. Then he leant over to take the picture from me, studying it carefully while he shielded it from the rain.

'I remember her fight. She lost, right?'

'She did. Via stoppage, halfway through the last round.'

'I remember thinking she wasn't cut out for it. I think I even told her, at one of the training sessions I attended. Too glamorous. She wasn't there for the boxing, just for the Instagram pictures.'

'But you let her fight anyway?'

'She did well, in the end. Tough opponent, could have gone either way. She proved me wrong.'

'But you don't remember her being there that night, at the party?'

'Hmm... now you mention it, maybe I do. I don't throw events like that very often, so when I do I let my hair down, know what I mean? But, yeah, I think maybe I spoke to her for a while. She was still sore about what I'd said to her, so she came over to have a moan.'

'What did she say?'

'All I can remember is her getting upset, and saying something about all older men being arseholes, or something like that. No, not arseholes.' He chuckled suddenly, the wan sunlight glinting off the metal in his mouth, making him seem like something robotic. '*Douchebags.* I remember that made me laugh. But I don't think she was really talking about me.'

'So who was she talking about?'

'Someone who'd hurt her, I suppose. I wish I could help you more.'

He returned to his digging, leaving me standing there in the rain, thinking.

9

Isaac swirled the liquid in his glass theatrically. 'My first issue is you referring to me as a "*sound technician*". Can't I be "director of audio architecture" or "master editor-in-chief" or something?'

'I thought you'd appreciate the shout-out.'

He sniffed haughtily, and drained the wine in a single gulp. They were in Napier's apartment, eating takeaway Chinese food after the lasagne she'd attempted to prepare had emerged looking more like a slab of tarmac. She was supposed to be off the booze for the boxing training, but the fight was still a good few weeks away, and a couple of glasses wouldn't hurt.

Which meant she probably shouldn't have just started on their third bottle.

'So what's the other issue, you ungrateful bastard?'

Isaac looked momentarily confused, squinting as though his derailed train of thought might reappear before his eyes. 'Oh yeah.' His expression transformed into something more serious. 'Your fight. I think it's weird that you haven't mentioned it on the show.'

Napier frowned. 'Why?'

'Three episodes in, and you're meeting with the guy who

organises the bloody events. It will sound really odd if you drop it in much later: "oh, and by the way, I'm actively training with Tony for a charity boxing match." It seems a bit dodgy, like you've got an undisclosed interest or something.'

'But I'm not training with him.'

'You know what I mean.'

'I just don't want to mix myself into this too much. It's Katrin's story, not mine.'

'It's too late. You're already part of the narrative, Elaine. You can't hide from it. You've even moved here, for Christ's sake – the police's case file probably has your name in it.'

She felt a chill drift through her at those words. Perhaps she *was* taking her interest in this case too far. Unravelling Katrin's last movements felt like following in the footsteps of a ghost.

'I don't doubt it,' she said, smiling as she tried to disguise how much Isaac had unsettled her. 'I tried to speak to the lead officer on the case, but she stonewalled me of course. I just wanted to know whether she even knew about the party on the night Katrin vanished, but she wasn't interested.'

'What's her name?'

'Yvonne Demetriou. DI then, still a DI now – I guess failing to crack the case didn't help her promotion prospects. Maybe that's why she's sour about me sticking my nose in.'

'Well, just wait till you've got tens of thousands of listeners – your fans will go and break down her office door for you.'

Napier laughed, finishing her own glass before she poured them both a top-up. Still reflecting on his words, she glanced around the apartment she was renting. She'd only been there for a couple of months, but already the place was unmistakeably hers, the shelves lined with ornaments, trinkets and books, the walls decorated with old framed posters of bands like Pixies and The Breeders, and David Bowie dressed as Jareth the Goblin King in *Labyrinth*. There were also a few of her own paintings, expressionist portraits of friends she displayed with a mixture of pride and self-conscious embarrassment. She'd had a go at painting Isaac once; his assessment of the result was that it 'looked like something out of *The X-Files*'. ('So it's highly accurate then,' had been her reply, of course.)

Her Alexa Dot, cycling through a nineties Spotify playlist, coughed up Everything but the Girl, which seemed somehow appropriate. She realised that they were sharing something resembling a comfortable silence, which wasn't spoiled even by her becoming aware of its existence.

'So what's going out next?' Isaac asked eventually.

'The one with Katrin's parents. Although I'm worried it'll seem a bit... I don't know... tactless.'

'What, like you're trying too blatantly to tug on people's heartstrings?'

'I suppose so. They sounded so sad... and so thankful for my help. I just want to make sure I'm doing this for the right reasons.'

'Are you?'

His question startled her. She knew there were a number of motives behind her project. She loved listening to true crime podcasts, and her journalistic investigation skills seemed like a perfect fit for such an endeavour. She'd heard about Katrin's disappearance from Fiona, another former colleague, when she'd floated the podcast idea to try to fend off the inevitable question: 'So what are you up to since leaving the *Chron*?'

Jobless and depressed, thanks. Meeting you for coffee is the first time I've been outside for nearly a fortnight.

Fiona had mentioned a story she remembered reporting on, an Icelandic girl who had mysteriously vanished. Napier had followed up, and slowly the unsolved case of Katrin Gunnarsdottir had sunk its hooks into her brain.

And, of course, there was Sam.

'I don't know,' she said. 'It just seems like they're an essential part of the story.'

'Then go for it. It might be her story, but it's your show.'

Napier nodded, chewing her lip. 'I'll send it to you for editing tomorrow. There's a part I want you to take out, where her mother asks me whether I have children of my own. It's not relevant.'

'You really are determined to edit yourself out of this, aren't you?'

Napier shrugged. Silence enveloped them again, suddenly less comfortable.

'Maybe I'll leave that part alone in the first cut, and then you can see what you reckon,' he persisted.

Another shrug. Around her, the apartment felt oppressive, the detritus she had crammed into it seeming like the wreckage of a life lived badly.

'Whatever you think,' she replied eventually. 'You're the master editor-in-chief of audio architecture, after all.'

Isaac laughed, and reached across to top up her wine glass. The last drops dribbling from the bottle reminded her of sand in an hourglass.

10

EXTRACT FROM SAMANTHA NAPIER'S DIARY

Dear Phil,

Thank you so so much for taking my heart, crushing it, then trampling on the still-bleeding remains. Thank you also for picking a night when I was physically there in person to witness you going with someone else behind my back – the image of you kissing that acne-faced freak Hannah will now be forever burned into my retinas. Finally, thank you for the locket you bought me for my 13th birthday last year, which is now at the bottom of the canal.

Going back through this diary, I counted fifty-six times I had written your name, or your initials, sometimes next to mine in a heart with an arrow through it. So I suppose I owe you another thank you, for finally making me realise how stupid I was. You'll be pleased to know that every one of them has now been scribbled out. I've also thrown away the scrapbook I made of all our photos together, which made me cry, because we look so happy and so perfect. But now I know it was all bullshit, and that you never really cared.

Anyway, I am now moving on to plotting my revenge, trying to decide which boy(s) I'm going to get off with in front of you. I can't decide whether to pick the ugliest geeks in school, or maybe just your best friends? (Don't worry, I'm not serious — unlike some people I'm not a complete slag.)

But there IS someone who can maybe take my mind off you for a while... and he's going to be there on Friday night, so we'll just have to see what sparks end up flying. Not only is Stu better looking than you, but he's older and bigger and he does karate, so you'd better just stay out of our way if you don't want to get your stupid gawky teeth smashed in.

Yours hatefully,

Sam x

PS I hope you and that spotty bitch are very happy together.

11

PODCAST EPISODE 5:

THE PARENTS

In Iceland, surnames work differently to what we're used to in Britain. Children take their father's first name and add 'sson' or 'sdottir' to it – so Katrin Gunnarsdottir is literally 'the daughter of Gunnar'. Her father is Gunnar Olafsson, 'the son of Olaf', and so on. This means that Icelandic parents and their children usually all have different surnames.

'It's a nightmare getting through security when we go on holiday,' laughed her mother, Anna, whose surname is Kristjansdottir. I am speaking to them via a Skype connection, so apologies if the sound quality is a little below par. This interview was recorded several weeks ago, when I first began to be interested in investigating Katrin's case, because I wanted to ensure that Gunnar and Anna were supportive of this podcast before we proceeded any further.

'The police have done nothing, so any new approach is fine with me.' That's Gunnar, a former construction worker and a man of few words. He was scathing about the official investigation, and had, at one point, even hired his own private detective to look into Katrin's disappearance.

'Yes. If your programme helps us find out what happened to our daughter, we are very happy to help.'

'I just need you both to know that I'll leave no stone unturned in search of the truth. We'll need to look at Katrin's friendships, her private life, even her relationships. There is a risk that we'll uncover things you didn't know about your daughter; things that might shock or upset you.'

There was a long pause, and I wondered for a moment if the signal had dropped out. Then Gunnar replied, his voice hollow and emotionless, like some part of him had been scooped out.

'So be it.'

When I asked them for their fondest memories of their daughter, Anna sounded almost thrilled to be given an opportunity to reminisce. Her love for Katrin is so clear in her voice, like a distant beacon cutting through the fog of her grief.

'Katrin was such an inquisitive child. Fearless, really. We first visited the UK when she was six, and I remember taking her to London Zoo. They were feeding the tigers, which meant the animals were temporarily moved into a separate holding area, and you could watch them through the glass or plastic or whatever it was. Katrin was pressed right up against it, and the tiger – this gigantic, terrifying creature with sharp teeth and claws – was there on the other side, staring back at her, pawing at the glass.

'I remember the other people around us gasping in awe, terrified at seeing such a monster up close; but Katrin wasn't afraid at all. I remember her pressing her hands against the glass and asking me if she could get inside so she could stroke it properly.

'I think that is maybe the day she fell in love with your country. For as long as I can remember, she always wanted to go there again, and when she realised it was possible through her studies, that became her unshakeable plan. I hear about a lot of academically gifted children losing their way in adolescence, because they don't know what they want to do with their lives and get bored in school, but for Katrin there was always a really clear goal: a place in a UK university.

'I realise how blessed we were to have such a wise, brave and loving daughter.'

'Still, it must have been very hard for you both when she moved away.'

Anna and Gunnar have no other children, and have since moved out of the family home where Katrin grew up. They live just outside of Reykjavik now, in a town called Mosfellsbaer.

'No, not really. It warms your heart to see your children doing well in life. Do you have children, Ms Napier?'

I told her that I don't.

'You hear about some parents who try to keep their children close by; to clip their wings, as I believe is your saying. I did not understand this at all. A mother's job is to give her children care and protection while they are in the nest; but then they must fly away, and make their own way in the world. Or at least, that is what I believed, back then.'

'And has that changed?'

'I don't know. I just know that I had something so precious... and then I let it out of my sight, and before I knew it, it was lost.'

I felt such enormous pity for Anna at that moment that it took me a few seconds to compose myself. 'One thing I hear a lot about in cold cases like this is the idea of 'closure'; that people can only truly move on when they learn the truth of what happened. Do you believe that?'

'I don't know. We've tried, for what it's worth. To move on, I mean. I have an online business selling arts and crafts. It's actually been surprisingly successful.'

'And what about you, Gunnar?'

'I'm retired. Anna tells me I need a hobby other than drinking.'

I laughed politely, even though I wasn't sure whether this was supposed to be a joke.

'Forgive me for this question, but I must ask – do you believe Katrin is still out there somewhere? And if so, do you have a message for her?'

'Just that we miss you very much, sweetheart. You are our little angel. Your father and I will never stop loving you.'

'What about you, Gunnar?'

There was a long pause before Gunnar spoke. When he did, his voice was as cold as the glaciers that have made his homeland famous.

'I do not believe she is out there. I believe somebody murdered our baby girl, and I pray that you can catch them, so they can be punished mercilessly.'

The jarring contrast between their words stuck with me for days afterwards. At first I found Gunnar's response shocking, ruthless even, but if anything it is those chilling words that have strengthened my determination to solve this mystery, and to bring Katrin's parents the closure I talked about.

I looked at Anna's website earlier this week, and have included the link in the show notes. Her work is delightful, including little figurines made from local pebbles and clothes pegs, knitted teddies and grinning gnomes.

The sort of gifts a mother might buy for her daughter.

12

_____

Of all the problems with getting older, Napier's biggest one was that drinking sessions seemed to take a lot longer to recover from. She and Isaac had polished off a fourth bottle of wine before he'd finally excused himself to stumble into a Ryde. 'Let me know when you get home,' she'd said, and then promptly fallen asleep, fully clothed and face down in her bed.

That had been two nights ago. Yesterday had been entirely sacrificed to that cruellest of gods, the atrocious hangover, and she had diligently observed all of His rituals; the groaning resurrection, the coffee, the paracetamol, the crushing self-loathing, the feeble attempt to get some work done, the defeated crawl back into bed. Her sole accomplishment had been to text Isaac and establish that, yes, somehow, he was indeed still alive, although in no better shape than she was.

Today she'd been hoping to be fully recuperated. She needed to be; she had two days of work to catch up on, updating case notes, making calls, scheduling social media posts, and trying to get in touch with the private eye Katrin's father had once hired. But that was the comparatively easy part. The real reason she needed to be totally on her game was that in the evening she had another sparring session with Martina.

Now the diminutive instructor stood across the ring from her, jaw set in a grim expression that suggested that, although this might be part of a training programme, absolutely no mercy would be shown. The Italian's gloves were raised in a guard that looked as rigid as an iron cage. Napier swallowed heavily, moving the gum shield around her mouth with her tongue. She still wasn't used to wearing it, and found it difficult to breathe properly; coupled with the claustrophobic tightness of the head guard, she was suddenly overwhelmed by a sense of suffocation, fear scrabbling inside her chest like a trapped animal.

More than anything, she felt *cornered*.

Not a good place to be while still nursing a two-day hangover.

'Okay. We do two minutes,' came the trainer's voice, as absolute as a death knell. Napier kept waiting for all the techniques she had learned to date to click into place, but instead the phrases just swam inside her head, hollow and meaningless, driftwood on a sea of panic.

Keep your guard up

Stay on your toes

Get in, strike, get out

Rotate your body

Use your combos

Block

Hook

Uppercut

Jab

<u>Cross</u>

The round seemed to last far longer than two minutes, but also to be over instantly; it was as though time had fragmented and then coalesced, waiting for an endless and mocking eternity before crystallising into a blunt slab of pain driven right into her face.

One moment she was piling forward with a flailing haymaker that Martina avoided easily, flinging a bruising right into Napier's ribs like a reprimand. Then the Italian was throwing jabs, probing her guard, stinging her with another body shot that brought her gloved hands instinctively down to protect her kidneys.

Seconds later she was down on one knee, holding a glove across her nose and right eye. They felt as though they were simultaneously numb and throbbing, frozen and on fire.

'Let me help you,' Martina was saying as she loosened Napier's headgear. 'Spit out your gum shield.'

Napier obeyed, the mouth guard plopping wetly onto the canvas. *At least there's no blood mixed with the saliva*, she thought as she began to remove her gloves. She glanced at Martina, hunkered down next to her, through her one open eye.

'Not bad for a beginner?' was the best she could muster.

The Italian's eyes narrowed. 'You were drinking this weekend, yes?'

Napier tilted her head backwards, grimacing as she held her fingers to the bridge of her nose. The skin there felt tender and swollen, the cartilage beneath it crunchy and sore.

'Yes, but you didn't have to smash my face in.'

'I'm sorry if I hurt you,' Martina said evenly. 'But you are not good enough. You must get better, and quickly. You will fight in less than two months. This will not be against your friend. This will be against another fighter, someone who wants to... How you say...? Smash your face in. And yet you go and drink.'

Her nose wasn't broken, but the swelling wouldn't be pretty. Thank God she was a podcaster and not a TV presenter.

'It is time you must take this more seriously,' Martina continued.

'Okay, okay, point taken. You could have told me that without turning me into the fucking Elephant Man.'

'I will cancel the rest of the session. Go and put ice on your face, and come back tomorrow.'

'But we don't have a session tomorrow.'

'Now we do. Is an emergency. We will spar again. Free of charge. So be ready for me, this time.'

Martina rose gracefully, powering upwards from a squatting position as though her legs were pistons. Napier watched as she turned away, removing her gloves and climbing nimbly out of the ring, her dyed pink hair barely out of place.

Then Napier called to her. 'Martina?'

The Italian turned, her face as neutral and detached as always. 'Yes?'

'Did you say you had another fight coming up?'

'Ahh, yes. Is this weekend actually. I will fight on the undercard.'

'Is it still possible to get tickets?'

To Napier's surprise, Martina smiled, the expression seeming out of place on the fighter's usually glacial features. She looked suddenly younger, just a typical twenty-something enjoying her life.

Like Katrin.

'Yes, of course! I can get one for you tomorrow.'

'Can I bring my friend?'

'Sure! Two tickets. I will see if I can get you front row.'

'How much is that?'

Martina waved a finger. 'No, no, is my pleasure. I will buy for you.'

Napier forced a smile back, wondering at the paradox of this pretty young woman and her life of violence.

Something alluring. Something that had called out to Katrin.

She thought about Tony Weaver, driving his spade into the dirt, proudly wearing his grisly medallion.

Perhaps violence claims all of us, eventually.

She rolled out of the ring and headed for the changing rooms, the pain in her nose subsiding into a dull ache.

13

PODCAST EPISODE 6:

THE PRIVATE EYE

In the last episode we heard from Gunnar and Anna, Katrin's parents. Remember me mentioning that Gunnar had hired a private detective to investigate their daughter's disappearance? Wim Hellendoorn, a Dutch PI who has been based in the UK since 1996, was so moved by the case that he continued to work on it, for free, for months after the official end of his investigation. Yet he was never able to solve the mystery.

Today, I went to meet him.

'What the hell happened to you?'

That's Wim, referring to my freshly-acquired black eye. He sat opposite me at his desk, frowning at my injury. I hope he won't mind me saying that, as well as sounding like his compatriot Rutger Hauer, he also looks a lot like the actor in his later years... if Rutger had perhaps put on a few extra pounds.

'I'm training for a charity boxing match. Katrin did one the year before she disappeared, so I wanted to put myself through the same process, to see if it threw up any fresh leads.'

'It doesn't look like you're very good at it.'

Wim retired two years ago, and is now in his early sixties. I don't think tact is his strong point.

'You should see the other guy. Anyway, enough about me; it's great to finally meet you. Why don't you tell the listeners a bit about yourself – and how you got involved in Katrin's case.'

Wim sighed deeply and sank back into his chair, a cracked red leather monstrosity that looks as though it's been salvaged from a reservoir. We were in his office, which is actually a downstairs room in the house he used to share with his former partner. The house is a dilapidated relic in the leafy suburb of Sydenham, surrounded by trees at the end of a winding dirt track. The office itself doesn't seem to have changed since his detective days, except that it now functions more like a study and all-purpose man-cave. It looks like an amalgamation of every detective's office in every movie I've ever seen: he has framed newspaper cuttings on the walls, filing cabinets everywhere, and even an old-fashioned magnifying glass on his desk.

'I used to work in security back in the nineties, and we won a big contract in the UK. That's when I met Ian, who was once my long-suffering other half. We were a lot quieter about our relationship back then, of course. I moved here to be with him, quit the job and opened this detective agency – and it was the best thing I ever did. Until Katrin.'

Wim has a larger-than-life personality, and is clearly something of a showman. When he paused, I half expected him to remove a bottle of Scotch from the desk drawer and pour us both a glass, or maybe offer me a cigar.

'Her father contacted me in 2013, friend of a friend thing, you know. My case resolution rate is second to none. At least, it was then.'

His gaze drifted off for a moment, panning around the newspaper clippings and cardboard archiving boxes. I wondered about this man's past and the cases he had investigated, imagining a blurry reflection of myself in twenty years' time.

'He asked me if I would look into the disappearance of his daughter. They couldn't really afford my rates, but I felt sorry for him, so I said okay, and gave him a discount. In the end I didn't charge them a penny.'

'Is that because you felt like you'd failed him?'

I was worried he might be offended by the question, but his answer was immediate and unambiguous.

'Yes.'

'What do you think made this case different? Why didn't your methods work on this occasion?'

'Damned if I know. If I'm honest, I think maybe it's because detective work is usually easy. There's a prime suspect, and they're *always* guilty. It's the jealous boyfriend, or the obsessive father, or the weird family friend. It's just your job to get the evidence, something to help the police build their case. Crimes are never committed by creepy strangers in a white van.'

'But you believe in the Coughing Man story?'

'I do. At the start I thought Marcus was the culprit, but this time I was wrong. I came to believe his story about the phone call with Katrin, and I even found a company that had the evil eye as their logo.'

This piqued my interest. 'Who were they?'

'A security firm, would you believe? My old line of work. Focus Security Solutions. They've since been swallowed up into one of the bigger contractors, but they were a start-up at the time. I ended up interviewing every single one of their operatives. But it came to nothing: there was no one matching the Coughing Man's description, no one without an alibi.'

'But you're convinced they're involved.'

'Occam's razor. What's the simplest explanation in the circumstances? The Ryde driver is in the clear, and the suitcase is inside the apartment. Therefore she went there, dropped it off, and *then* was taken. Who would do that? The boyfriend's car was in the garage, like he said – I checked – so he couldn't have got there unless he took a Ryde of his own. But then what would he do with the body, without a vehicle? Those premises were thoroughly searched, as well as all the surrounding streets and parks.'

'Maybe he borrowed one from the garage?'

'I checked that too.'

'Or rented one?'

'Checked. No records of anyone renting a car under his name, and no suspicious payments from his bank account.'

'What about if he used cash and a false name? Or what if he was already at her place when she called him?'

'It still leaves him with a body to dispose of, without a vehicle.'

'Maybe he had an accomplice.'

'Look at it another way – how would he benefit from the crime? The only explanation for Marcus killing her would be a crime of passion, and crimes of passion leave a mess behind; they don't come pre-planned with accomplices and getaway cars.'

'Okay. But why does that mean it had to be the Coughing Man? You couldn't find anyone else with a motive?'

'Well, there were rumours. There always are, with pretty girls. You must know that.'

'You're too kind.'

'I try. Sometimes you need to be able to turn on the charm in this job.'

He gave me a somewhat melancholy smile.

'But seriously, Wim – couldn't someone else have come to her apartment, someone she knew and trusted?'

'The only other possibility was a guy she was supposedly seeing on the side.'

'An older guy?'

'That's right. But I never found out who. I'm not convinced it was anything more than workplace gossip.'

'It was someone from Triton Homes?'

'Perhaps. A couple of her close friends told me about a mysterious "Mr Wolf" she used to talk about. But none of the male executives had anything like that as a surname, and all of them had cast-iron alibis for that night.'

I took the names of the friends. The list of people I need to talk to keeps growing. What's interesting is that Wim knew them instantly, off the top of his head, without having to consult any of his reams of notebooks and files.

'How did Gunnar react when you couldn't give him an answer?'

Wim gave another long sigh. 'Our relationship deteriorated, to be honest. Even when I continued to work on the case for free, it got to the point where he wouldn't return my calls. In some ways, that investigation heralded the beginning of the end for me. My casebook started to dwindle, and I was spending half my nights just sitting in here, poring over my notes about Katrin, drinking, not earning any money. Then Ian left, and that just meant more work, and more drinking. Then I had my heart attack, and realised I'm not the physical specimen I once was. So I admitted defeat, and retired.'

He grinned lopsidedly, and then to my complete non-surprise he really *did* produce a bottle of booze from his desk drawer. It was genever rather than whiskey, true to his Dutch roots, but still. I declined a glass and he gave me a 'suit yourself' shrug, pouring himself a liberal measure.

'So you really think it's the boyfriend, eh?'

I said in an earlier episode that I would offer no opinions in this podcast. But, just like Hellendoorn himself, there comes a point when you just have to choose what, and who, to believe.

'No. I trust Marcus too.'

'The case ruined his life.'

I looked at the detective, surrounded by the nostalgic remnants of his once-successful agency, of his relationship, and I wondered whether that statement could also apply to him.

'What if I've got a new lead for you, Wim?'

This is when I told him about the party, about Jamal and Tony, both of whom he had never heard of. For a while he just stared at me, offering a rueful version of that uneven smile. I thought he might be about to drain the entire bottle of liquor, but instead, he carefully put it away.

'Years I worked on that case. And you've stumbled on a breakthrough on pretty much your first day.'

'Call it beginner's luck.'

'If you're not careful, you're going to tempt me out of retirement.'

'I wouldn't want to put any more strain on your heart.'

At this point, the grin widened, and – you guessed it – he produced a box of cigars.

'Don't worry. That old thing broke ages ago.'

I shared a Cuban with him before I left. His expression as he sat there, surrounded by memories and swirling smoke, seemed a lot happier than when I arrived.

14

EXTRACT FROM MARSH GROVE GAZETTE, 1992

SEARCH CONTINUES FOR LOCAL TEENAGER

The Marsh Grove community is still reeling after the disappearance of 13-year-old Samantha Napier, who is still missing after failing to return to her family home on Friday night.

It is believed she visited Ashgate Park, a known haunt for local youths where there were several rumoured sightings of her, but police have been unable to establish her movements later that evening.

Police yesterday released from custody a 17-year-old male, who had been assisting them with their enquiries. Fears for Samantha Napier's safety are increasing with each passing day.

Samantha's mother, Michelle Napier, said: 'Sam was the light of my life. Things haven't been perfect at home since her dad passed away, but I honestly don't think she would just run away like this. Her little sister and I are in pieces. Please, Sammy, if you're reading this, just come home and everything will be forgiven.'

Police have appealed for anyone with information about the teenager's whereabouts to contact them immediately.

15

'So… Wim is on the team now?' Isaac looked bemused.

'Well, let's not get carried away,' Napier replied. 'He says he's happy to help out wherever he can, and doesn't expect us to pay him. So he might come in very handy. And if nothing else, what a great character to feature on the show!'

'Yeah, just what I need in my life: another lunatic.'

Isaac had already grilled her about the black eye. She had dismissed his concerns, of course, finding his 'worried grown-up' routine quite endearing.

'You'll see plenty more of them tonight.'

'I cannot *believe* I agreed to go to this thing with you. I don't even like violence!'

'Think of it as research.'

The event, named 'Caged Fury', was taking place in a leisure centre in Brentford. Martina had told them to arrive at 8pm, as she would be appearing about halfway through the show's five-hour running time. They had got there a little early, chatting while they queued to be patted down by security staff. She realised she had never given a second thought to the companies that provided that service, to the faceless men and women who hovered menacingly at the entrances to clubs, gigs and sporting events, guarding the doors like ancient soldiers at the castle gates.

The presence of those hulking sentries was reassuring, but only for as long as you trusted them.

Hellendoorn had interviewed every operative of Focus Security Solutions. But what if he'd missed something?

It was a young crowd, and Napier felt all of her thirty-eight years as they descended into the basement sports hall, which had been transformed into something like a nightclub for the evening; music boomed through scattered speakers, and coloured spotlights danced around the walls and across the crowd, many of whom were wearing cocktail dresses or dinner jackets, laughing and chatting as they drank at their tables or stocked up at the bar. There was even a food stall selling curry and samosas.

'Bloody hell. Now I feel underdressed as well as old,' Isaac grumbled, having to raise his voice to be heard over the thumping bass.

In the centre of the seething, boozing mass was the cage. An imposing hexagonal structure made from chain-link fence panels, it looked like something lifted straight out of a dystopian sci-fi movie. It was larger than Napier had expected, yet somehow also more claustrophobic, and she tried to imagine being sealed inside. The fights this evening would be longer than her own upcoming event, and with very different rules; MMA competitors had three five-minute rounds in which they were permitted to punch, kick, elbow and knee their opponent (no headbutts or groin strikes were allowed), or to utilise their arsenal of submission holds as they attempted to defeat their rival via stoppage, submission – 'tapping out' as it was known – or judges' decision.

They watched as a ring announcer took up a position in the centre of the cage, and the music faded.

'Ladies and gentlemen, please welcome the competitors for your next bantamweight bout!' he bellowed in a voice reminiscent of an eighties radio DJ. Then he paused as music blared, an indecipherable and nasty hip-hop track, while the big screen over the entrance ramp lit up with an image of the first combatant. A handsome young man of Middle Eastern descent pouted into the camera, his body like a chiselled statue, hair perfectly tousled.

'Introducing first, hailing from Luton, with a record of two wins and only one defeat... Gorgeous George Grazi!' The last syllable was drawn out for what felt like an entire minute.

'It's a bit like WWF,' Isaac whispered in her ear.

'It's called WWE now,' she corrected him. 'They got sued by the panda.'

He raised an eyebrow as if to say 'how on earth do you know that?', and Napier winked as she turned to watch Grazi's entrance. He emerged surrounded by an entourage of five other men, his face hidden beneath a sweat towel. The walk to the cage door was short, but he dragged it out for as long as he possibly could before removing the towel to be checked and patted down by the refereeing crew, who were searching for loose jewellery, buckles or zips that could inadvertently injure his opponent. This process took a long time, and Grazi's music finished before he even made it into the cage; but he didn't seem to mind. He faced each side of the arena in turn, arms outstretched as he presented himself confidently to the crowd. They cheered and whooped in adulation, seemingly appreciating his showmanship.

'Arrogant twat,' muttered Isaac.

'You're just jealous,' Napier replied as the announcer stepped back into the spotlight.

'And his opponent, hailing from Poznan, Poland, with a record of seventeen bouts and twelve victories... the Glacier, Oskar Lazarski!'

The contrast between Lazarski and his rival couldn't be any more jarring. Where Grazi was boyish, Lazarski looked battle-hardened, a shaven-headed and grizzled ring veteran; where Grazi was short and stocky, Lazarski was gangly, his arms almost simian as they hung by his sides during his entrance walk; where Grazi courted the crowd, Lazarski was silent and sullen, listening intently to one of his cornermen who whispered in his ear all the way to the cage. He had a Polish flag draped across his back, and his music was a wordless cacophony that might have been Aphex Twin.

Napier scanned the programme they had picked up upon entering, and saw that her trainer was up next in a flyweight contest. This match was her one chance to get accustomed to the rules before watching Martina compete.

'I'll get the drinks in, since you clearly aren't offering,' grumbled Isaac, rising from his chair. The venue was small enough for every seat to have a good view of the action. 'Beer, wine or vodka?'

'Just a water for me, thanks,' Napier replied. He stared incredulously at her for a few moments as though doubting her sanity, then turned towards the bar with a shake of his head.

The fight started explosively, with Grazi trying to catch the taller man off guard with a flurry of strikes. The crowd shrieked, and Napier found herself swept along by the current of their euphoria; it wasn't bloodlust, not exactly, more a desire to see some *action*. Lazarski fended off the attack using long jabs and kicks to establish distance, and the first round petered out into what felt like a stalemate.

Isaac reappeared, carrying two plastic cups as well as a bottle of water. He mumbled apologies as he squeezed past the others seated on their row, his Grateful Dead T-shirt contrasting hilariously with their James Bond bow ties and little black (and white, and gold) numbers.

'I got you a double in case you change your mind, Mother Teresa.'

'Not interested, mate. Got to stay sober until my fight.'

He gave her another one of his disapproving looks, before draining the first cup in a single gulp. The second round had started, the tempo similar at first to the cagey, slow pace of the first, before Lazarski struck about one minute in. With the speed of a cobra, he sidestepped a strike from Grazi and wrapped his long limbs around his opponent, dragging him backwards and down onto the mat. Grazi tensed and struggled, but Lazarski held on grimly, his legs locked around the younger man's waist. It was like watching a sea monster dragging a freighter under the waves.

'This is boring,' said Isaac after a while. 'How many matches do we have to sit through?'

Napier checked the programme once again; they had already missed six bouts prior to this one, with another two to go after Martina's contest. Then there was an interval, and then the five fights that comprised the main card.

'Just a couple more,' she lied.

'Who's winning?'

'Just bloody watch it and then you'd know.'

Grazi managed to survive the round, but wore a pained expression when he emerged from the tangle of arms and legs, his breathing heavy. Lazarski looked as coldly unperturbed as ever; it was easy to see how he had obtained his nickname.

'So what was the point of that?' Isaac asked through a mouthful of the crisps he had produced from somewhere. 'He just hugged him for the entire round.'

'I suppose he's just wearing him down, or trying to make him submit. I'm not an expert.'

'I'm supporting the lanky one.'

'I'm sure he's thrilled.'

The final round started with a renewed explosion of offence from Grazi, who had been admonished by his coach during the break. Lazarski dodged around the cage, surprisingly nimble despite his height, but took a right hand to the chin that seemed to unnerve him for the first time. The crowd roared, and Napier found herself shouting too, struck by how easily the narrative of the match had unfolded. Just ten minutes in and there was an established crowd favourite, plucky and confident, battling bravely against a taller and more experienced aggressor; a simple story told with virtually no words.

The fight ended with Lazarski mounting a counter-offensive of his own, a hail of kicks and knees whose viciousness was belied by his unflustered deportment. At the final bell, Grazi raised his arms as if convinced of his victory, while Lazarski just ambled back towards his coaches, almost as though he didn't care about the result at all.

'I think the skinny one won. Definitely a points victory,' said Isaac.

'I thought you didn't like it?'

'Well, I thought I might as well make an effort. Want a crisp?'

'No thanks,' she replied, turning her nose up at the proffered prawn cocktail snack. 'Did they have any other flavours?'

'I didn't get them from the bar; I brought them myself. It's only 50p for a multipack at Home Bargains.'

She rolled her eyes and turned to watch the announcement of the fight's result: Lazarski won on points in a unanimous decision. The big man celebrated with surprising enthusiasm, ignoring a few boos from the crowd as he hugged his coaches and pumped the air with a still-gloved fist. But Napier was watching the crestfallen Grazi, whose earlier confidence seemed to have completely vaporised. He was a forlorn figure as he exited the cage, and she wondered about these people, these fighters who expended so much of their blood and sweat during the intense months of training, making so much sacrifice. And for what? A tiny sliver of time that could make or break their careers, shatter their self-confidence, dissolve their entire sense of identity.

What would Grazi do with the rest of his evening?

How would Napier feel if she lost her own fight?

How had Katrin felt?

She realised there were a thousand questions she wanted to ask the missing girl.

Isaac, already looking a little tipsy after his two double vodka tonics, made another trip to the bar as the ring announcer reappeared to introduce the next bout.

The other girl was out first, a Hungarian of similar height and build to Martina, her long dark hair braided in tight corn rows, her skin so pale it seemed almost white under the glaring lights. She used John Carpenter's theme from *Halloween* as her entrance song, her focused expression no less terrifying than the music as she stalked towards the cage. Napier began to worry about her coach, then remembered their sparring bout a few days previously, and changed her mind.

Martina came out to 'Smack My Bitch Up' by The Prodigy, drawing a snort of laughter from Isaac. Her coach's face was as stern and serious as usual, until she spotted some of her friends in the crowd, and grinned as she waved at them. Napier managed to catch her eye and offer her a thumbs-up gesture, which Martina returned with a smile.

'So that's the woman I have to beat up for giving you a black eye?' slurred Isaac. 'I think I could take her.'

'Trust me – you couldn't,' replied Napier, eyes glued to the cage as the two fighters exchanged final words with their coaches.

Then the bell sounded, and Martina pulverised her opponent mercilessly.

Punches, knees, kicks, even a spinning back elbow all featured in her frenzied opening onslaught. The Hungarian was down inside the first minute, then again twenty seconds later. When she hit the deck a third time, the referee waved his hands to signal an abrupt end to the contest.

The crowd were hysterical, Napier and Isaac whooping and applauding along with them as Martina shook hands with her opponent and then celebrated with her coach. That's when Napier spotted him: Tony Weaver, in Martina's corner, grinning his silver smile. She shouldn't have been surprised – she already knew he ran Martina's promotion company – but seeing him there was somehow unnerving, as though one part of her life had bled into another, like in a dream.

'That's Tony,' she whispered to Isaac. 'The bloke with the teeth.'

'Fucking hell,' Isaac said. 'He looks scary.'

'He is.'

They watched the next couple of fights, two cautious men's contests that ended respectively in a points victory and a draw. By now, the well-oiled Isaac was enthralled by the action, but Napier couldn't help glancing at Weaver. The promoter was sitting in the opposite corner of the venue, a bored look on his face as he flicked through his phone. She wondered what she would do if he saw her there, and felt a hot sensation in her cheeks. It wasn't as though there had been anything untoward in their previous exchange; but, somehow, his presence made her feel uncomfortable.

Did she suspect him of some involvement in Katrin's disappearance?

Mercifully, there was no eye contact between them, no sign that he had spotted her. He slunk off before the interval while her gaze was momentarily drawn back to the cage. When the announcer informed the audience about the fifteen-minute break, she suggested to Isaac that they leave.

'But I'm just getting into it!' he protested as the lights went up and the pounding music started once again.

'Yeah, and you've also drank about eight double vodkas. I don't want to have to carry you into a taxi.'

He pulled a mock-sulking face and rose, stumbling as his foot caught on the chair leg. Together they headed back up the stairs towards the foyer; she felt as though she was emerging from some illicit, underground fight club, and again understood some of the appeal of this world to its participants and fans. Katrin's own desire to fight, like Napier's, was something complex, a compulsion that couldn't easily be explained.

As they headed towards the exit, she glanced to the side, down a partitioned-off corridor that presumably led to the fighters' changing rooms. Martina was leaning against the wall, now changed and showered, glowing with the thrill of her victory.

Leaning in to kiss her, drawn in by her arms locked around his waist, was Tony Weaver.

16

PODCAST EPISODE 7:

THE WOLFMAN

In the last episode I met Wim Hellendoorn, a private investigator who has spent years trying to track down the Coughing Man. He told me that he had interviewed a couple of Katrin's friends, and that they had mentioned another character, someone she called 'Mr Wolf'. I decided to track these friends down, to see if I could find out anything else about this lead.

At the time of her disappearance, they both worked for Triton Homes, as did most of Katrin's friends; apart from Marcus she had lost touch with those she had made at university, and back home in Iceland. I can't imagine how difficult it must have been for her to make the switch to a new country, learning a different language, building a new life from nothing.

The two friends in question have both since left Triton Homes, but they still live and work in London. I arranged to meet them in a coffee shop in the city centre, where they were happy for me to record the interview.

'Hi! Thanks for coming.'

'It's no problem.' That's Abigail Chikezie, who recently won a design award for her apartment building in Ealing.

'So how did you meet Katrin?'

'We were all on the same graduate programme.' That's Henry Wu, a Canadian who moved here at a similar time to Katrin. 'She was like me: foreign and shy!'

'You don't seem very shy.'

Henry was wearing an eye-wateringly gaudy floral print shirt. He just laughed; both of them seemed like easy-going, friendly people.

'Do you have any specific memories of Katrin, Abigail?'

'She was awesome. I wasn't really the most confident person back then, and she helped me come out of my shell. Nothing specific, really; I just remember that she was so much fun to be around, and you always felt like it was all about *you*, not her. She wasn't like other people our age. There were a lot of self-obsessed people on that grad programme.'

'Er, *hello*, I'm sitting right here?'

I joined them in chuckling. They hadn't seen each other for years, but it was easy to tell how close they had once been.

'What about you, Henry?'

'Oh, same. She was special. I remember how she used to talk with her hands all the time – really expressive with her gestures when she spoke. She used to sometimes knock things over or spill drinks because of it. I used to call her a klutz. Look, we're just so happy that you're doing this; it's so terrible to think that someone like her could just... go away, like that.'

'What do you think happened to her?'

'I think she was murdered. I'm sorry if that sounds cold, but I do. I think some horrible creep broke into her apartment and killed her.'

The apartment showed no signs of forced entry, or even of Katrin having spent her final night there, but of course people who aren't close to the case wouldn't know these specifics. I asked whether the horrible creep could be Mr Wolf; Henry looked at me blankly, but Abigail's face flashed with recognition.

'How did you know about that?'

'You mentioned him to Wim Hellendoorn, a private detective who interviewed you years ago. But he never found out who Mr Wolf was.'

Abigail frowned. 'Gosh, I'd almost forgotten... yes, that's right. She was seeing some guy – wait, am I allowed to say this?'

I explained that whatever she said would be used on the broadcast, and she seemed conflicted for a while, conferring briefly with Henry before she continued.

'Well, I don't want to make her sound... I know her boyfriend wasn't charged in the end, and I suppose he might be listening to this. He's probably suffered enough without hearing that she was seeing someone behind his back. But, she was, so there it is I suppose.'

'Who was he?'

'We never found out. She called him "Mr Wolf", like you said. It seemed to be like a game to her. When I asked why she called him that, she said it was because he was "big and bad". We got the impression he was an older man.'

'Someone from work?'

'She wouldn't say. We didn't really approve, so we just left it at that: this secret other life she was living that was none of our business.'

'But do you have any suspicions?'

Triton Homes started life as a family-owned company that has grown into a thriving corporate leviathan. With growth comes bureaucracy and middle management, and by the time Katrin came to work there it had adopted what is known as a matrix structure, where staff are effectively accountable to two bosses. In Katrin's case, these were the head of the residential division, and the head of the Hannibal Heights project itself. The idea was that there would be 'positive tension' between the two executives: one striving for standardisation, low cost and maximum profit, with the other motivated to appease the local planning committee, councillors and politicians, residents, and the general public. Katrin also had a direct line manager, as well as regular contact with the head of the graduate committee that was overseeing the programme. All of these people reported to the group's chief operating officer, who in turn reported to the CEO.

Back then, every single one of those people were men. Searching for Mr Wolf was like trying to find a needle in a particularly sexist haystack.

'No. I wish we could be more helpful.'

'Maybe you can. Do you know anything about a party at Hannibal Heights?'

This time Henry was the one who remembered something.

'I remember being there with her, yeah. It was pretty soon after the building had opened.'

'Do you remember whose party it was?'

'It was all party, party, party back then, you know? I was drunk basically every night for three years.'

'Try to remember, Henry. The party I'm talking about took place the night she disappeared.'

'No, that can't be right. I'd remember... but then, it was weeks before we found out what had happened to her. She just stopped coming to work, and there were all sorts of rumours flying around: she'd gone back to Iceland, she was off work with meningitis, she'd had a mental breakdown and wouldn't leave her flat... it was crazy.'

'But you said you think you remember the party. Do you recall who was there?'

'I just remember going to that fucking creepy building. Oops, am I allowed to swear?'

'I can bleep it out for you if you like.'

'No, don't worry. That's the right word for it: it really was fucking creepy. A museum with stuffed animals and pickled rabbits in jars – no thanks.'

'The party would have been at Tony Weaver's apartment, a boxing promoter – do you remember him?'

'Not really. I'm sorry. I know she was doing her boxing stuff around that time – we thought it was just another one of her mad phases.'

'Could *he* have been Mr Wolf?'

Tony certainly fits the description 'big and bad'.

'No, I don't think so. I got the invite from one of our other colleagues, who I think knew someone who knew someone who was going, and I remember him saying that he'd invited Katrin too. Katrin, if you're listening, I know you worked so hard on that building – I'm sorry I called it creepy!'

'Who was the colleague?'

I've decided to redact his name for now.

'… was just a guy we used to work with. He was really keen on Katrin at the time, always trying to get her to come out for drinks with him.'

'And what happened at the party?'

'I don't really remember. I feel like I spent most of the night just sitting around in someone's dingy front room, watching people smoking weed. Then suddenly Katrin was there, so I was like *Oh great, now it should liven up!* But I think I was just too wasted, and left soon after.'

'Did you leave with her?'

'I don't remember. I'm sorry. Oh God, are you telling me I abandoned her? And then someone…?'

'I'm not saying that at all, Henry. I just want to find out who else was there that night. Can you give me any other names?'

He couldn't. When I left them he seemed devastated, a shell of the flamboyant character that had first walked into the coffee shop. I felt terrible. But at least I'd found out about the other colleague, who I'm going to call 'L'; another name for my growing list. I thought about the 'secret other life' that Abigail had said Katrin was living, one that seemed at odds with the picture of a wholesome, hard-working young woman beloved by her parents, her boyfriend and her colleagues. I thought about taxidermy, about wild animals, and how the men in Katrin's life are beginning to seem more and more like circling predators.

Then when I got home, I found a message on our Facebook page.

First of all, I should thank everyone that's been contacting us, making suggestions and asking questions, and discussing the case. I'm delighted that we're generating so much interest and buzz around Katrin's story – and who knows, maybe raising its profile will encourage the police to formally reopen their investigation.

But this message made my blood run cold.

It was a post by someone calling themselves Lewis Carroll, all in lowercase. It read:

i was at the party too. katrin left at about 3am a white van picked her up. it was dirty and rusted and had an eye on the side.

As the real Lewis Carroll might have said: things are becoming curiouser and curiouser.

17

REFERRAL REPORT FOR ELAINE NAPIER, FORM 8A

Dear Mrs Napier,

We are sorry to inform you that Elaine misbehaved at school today, and had to be sent home. A group of boys were teasing her in the playground, and Elaine reacted by wrestling one of them to the ground and biting him in the neck, drawing so much blood that he had to be taken to hospital.

Whilst I acknowledge that Elaine is under immense stress given her sister's recent disappearance, and that other children tormenting her about this matter is not acceptable, neither can I tolerate violence like this under any circumstances.

Having spoken to Elaine, I believe she understands the severity of the incident, and that if she is upset by other children in future she should come directly to me. I am optimistic that this will prove to be an isolated occurrence, but would appreciate your support in reinforcing this message.

Yours sincerely,

Janet Lawton

Headteacher

18

It had been three days since Martina's fight, and Napier had already seen her coach for another sparring session, during which she got the distinct impression that the Italian was taking it easy on her. They'd talked about the fight, Martina modest yet clearly proud of such a decisive victory over a highly regarded opponent, but for some reason Napier hadn't felt able to ask about Tony Weaver. Martina's love life was none of her business, of course – except it was, because the whole reason she was training with Martina in the first place was because of Katrin. If her coach was dating someone who was somehow involved in the girl's disappearance, she owed it to Katrin to ask difficult questions.

But then, why did she feel so uncomfortable about Tony Weaver in the first place?

Because Katrin had attended a party at his apartment the night she died, that's why.

Because, when they'd met, he'd been enigmatic and guarded, quite possibly withholding something.

Because he was a violent man, a hulking grotesque who'd had his teeth replaced by a metal grille, and carried the old ones around on a chain round his neck.

Her brain felt like an overcooked stew as she drove towards Elephant and Castle, where she had arranged to meet Wim Hellendoorn. The area was yet another of London's regeneration zones, its centrepiece an enormous horseshoe-shaped intersection where she became stuck for a long time in grinding traffic. When she finally found Katrin's apartment building, Hellendoorn was already there, smoking a cigarette and leaning on a walking cane she was pretty sure he didn't need. The building loomed behind him, one of the many soulless new developments that continued to spring up all around the area, and she couldn't help thinking of sprouting weeds choking the life from a flower bed. Except she'd read about this particular flower bed, and how its infamous and now-demolished housing estates had deteriorated over the years into crime-ridden slums... but maybe that was just what the property developers wanted you to think. Either way, gentrification was a toxic word here, a moral grey area, a subject too big for her podcast.

'Nice journey?' asked Hellendoorn sarcastically as she climbed out of the car. His trench coat and fedora made him look like he was auditioning for the part of Columbo.

'Delightful,' she replied. 'Is there a law somewhere that says all private investigators have to dress like that?'

He wheezed a laugh, and sidled towards one of the other parked cars, a battered old saloon that might have been hiding white paint beneath its layers of grime. He struggled with the boot before eventually deploying a karate-chop motion to open it, revealing a large suitcase that was almost as decrepit as the car.

'For the experiment,' he announced.

Aside from the message from their mysterious 'informant', the Facebook page was starting to get a lot of engagement, and a number of listeners were challenging the assumption that the Ryde driver was innocent. Napier was still withholding his full name – John Hargreaves – on the show, but still she owed it to him and to their audience to test the timing herself, to make sure she agreed that six minutes was an impossible window in which he could have murdered Katrin, transported her suitcase upstairs, and disposed of her body.

'How shall we work this? Is there a superintendent or someone who can let us inside?'

Hellendoorn snorted, and produced a bunch of keys from the depths of a coat pocket. 'Skeleton key,' he explained.

'Are you sure this isn't illegal?'

'Oh, it definitely is. But it's all for a good cause.'

He opened the passenger door, and she slid into his car, grimacing at the stink of cigarette smoke. He rounded the bonnet and sagged into the driver's seat next to her.

'Okay, so I'm Hargreaves, and you're Katrin. We're both going to set a timer, and then I'm going to murder you.' She couldn't help but shudder a little at his words. 'The challenge is whether I can then dump your body, somewhere that no one could find it for five years, then get your suitcase all the way up to your apartment, then make it back down to drive the car away again, all inside six minutes. Or six minutes and twenty-two seconds, to be precise.' Once again, he extracted the information easily from the cavernous database of his memory.

'Presumably someone else is living in the apartment now?'

'Yeah, but I found out there's an unoccupied one on the same floor, and my key will get us inside.'

'That sounds *very* illegal.'

'Just don't mention it on your radio show.'

'It's a podcast.'

'Whatever.'

Napier started the timer on her phone, and Hellendoorn did

the same on his wristwatch. Then he mimicked putting his hands around her throat. She stiffened for a moment, but he didn't seem to notice.

Sam... is this what it was like?

His hands were thick and fleshy, and for a moment she felt a sliver of terror; the terror Katrin must have felt when she realised someone wanted to snatch her away from the world.

Like a white van driver, maybe. She hadn't told Hellendoorn about the tip-off yet.

'Let's say he used something, chloroform or whatever, to incapacitate her almost immediately. Then he'd need to get out of the car.' Hellendoorn circled quickly around the front of the vehicle to open the passenger door. Napier made a show of spilling out onto the pavement, which made him chuckle. 'Okay, very good. So let's say he lifted her up by the armpits, like this.' He heaved Napier into a standing position, grunting with the effort.

'I'm not *that* overweight, you monster.'

'No comment,' he retorted as he dragged her backwards towards a nearby bush. She wondered if anyone could see them, and hoped they didn't call the police. 'Now let's pretend he dumped her here. Which would be a huge risk, but let's imagine he comes back later in the evening, after he's clocked off, to dispose of the body properly.'

'Do you want me to fall in the bush?'

'No. Just get the suitcase.'

She hurried across to the car, and hauled it from the open boot. 'I thought it would be heavier than this.'

'She'd travelled fairly light,' he replied as they hurried towards the building. 'I checked the contents listed in the police records with her parents – they said nothing seemed to be missing. I've tried to load this with a similar weight to what hers would have been, so it's mainly full of some of my most tasteful Hawaiian shirts.'

They ran to the door and Hellendoorn jammed his key into the lock, leading them into a narrow lobby area. Mailboxes lined both walls, punctuated by doors halfway along on either side, with a lift facing them at the opposite end.

'That's a janitor's closet,' he said, gesturing to his right. 'This one is the stairs. Ladies first,' he said as he held open the left-hand door.

'I notice you're not offering to carry the suitcase,' she grumbled. 'Which floor is it?'

'Twelve. I'll meet you up there.' Then he turned and headed towards the lift doors, seeming to have suddenly acquired a limp.

She looked upwards at the spiralling steps above her, cursing him under her breath, and then ran up the stairs as fast as she could.

She reached the twelfth floor, utterly breathless, about four minutes later. She barged the door open to find Hellendoorn waiting for her at the opposite end of a long corridor. The walls were an insipid magnolia colour, reminding her of stained teeth. She struggled towards him across the threadbare beige carpet, swearing as she dropped the suitcase and had to turn around to pick it up.

'What took you so long?' he asked with a faint smirk, holding open the door to apartment 1211.

'Okay, okay,' she panted, wondering how much slower she'd have been without her recent boxing training. 'So we've proved he didn't take the stairs. But what about the lift?'

He glanced at his watch. 'It was nearly five minutes by the time I got up here, but we can try it again.'

'First let me see inside the apartment.'

'Be my guest.' He ushered her inside, allowing the door to close behind them.

The apartment was unfurnished, a pine-floored shell that seemed large and bright without the clutter of an inhabitant and their belongings. There was a single bedroom and bathroom, a closet containing the boiler and washing machine. The living room had a minuscule fitted kitchenette, and a small balcony overlooked the quiet street outside.

'Was Katrin's apartment laid out like this?'

He nodded. 'All the flats on this floor are identical.'

'Did you see inside hers?'

'They'd already found another tenant by the time Gunnar hired me. They let me take a look inside, but there wasn't much to see. When the police first searched it, her suitcase was on her bed, unopened, still full of all her holiday clothes, with her thick coat on top. Her passport was inside the case, and the bed was still freshly made.'

'But her purse and phone disappeared with her?'

'Yep. Along with her house keys.' Hellendoorn was looking around the place with an expression somewhere between nostalgia and revulsion.

'Which someone would have needed, so they could get inside to drop off the suitcase.'

'Unless they followed her up there. They could have followed her inside, then grabbed her after she dumped the case.'

'But how on earth could you do any of that in six minutes?'

Hellendoorn gave one of his all-purpose shrugs. 'Exactly. I've tried this from every angle. There's just no way it could be done. The fastest I could manage the round trip was seven minutes, and that was allowing absolutely zero time to do anything with Katrin herself. And remember that Hargreaves picked up his next ride straight away without another stop, and they didn't report anything suspicious.'

Six minutes. The same length of time as her boxing match. So brief as to be almost nothing. A speck of grit blown across the cosmos. A single life, ended in the blink of an eye, the flicker of a star, the flutter of a butterfly's wing.

'Did you interview Hargreaves?'

'I did. He was a mess when I met him. His wife left him soon after the investigation started, after four kids together. The police grilled him pretty hard for a while, and I think the experience broke him. He hadn't worked for weeks when I went to his house; he had a big beard and was really gaunt. The place was a dump, but I remember he had photos of his kids everywhere.'

She thought about Marcus Dobson. Like him, John Hargreaves was collateral damage; another life that had been blinked away on that cold night in January.

'Do you think he'd appear on the podcast? To clear his name, once and for all?'

'No harm in asking him. I'm pretty sure he moved away, so you'd have to track him down. If only there was a good private investigator you could hire to help you...' He gave a mischievous grin.

'I'm afraid it would have to be another unpaid gig, Wim.'

'I know, I know. You can pay me back when we crack this case and you're fending off big money sponsorship deals.'

Napier glanced around the apartment, feeling nothing; no sense whatsoever of its previous occupants, and certainly not of Katrin. Gripped by a sudden impulse, she turned and headed out into the corridor. She could hear Hellendoorn following behind her with the suitcase, his keys jingling as he locked the door behind them.

Instead of returning to the stairs or the lift, she instead followed the signs around the corner, stopping at a different door. She leaned forward to place her cheek against the wood, just below the silver digits of the apartment number. She wasn't listening, or even sure what she was doing. There was no peephole – the door was just a solid slab of pine, sturdy and unyielding.

It was the door to apartment 1206, the apartment that had once been Katrin's. She had lived there for over two years. Maybe some fragment of her essence was imprinted on the place, still lingering beneath the changing tenants, the deep cleans, the five years of wear and tear; the endless, inexorable cycle of the Earth.

The planet turned, the world moved on, people moved out, people moved in. People were born. People died.

Napier raised her hand and knocked twice on the door. There was no sound beyond it. The whole building seemed desolate, as though mourning its loneliness, grieving for the inhabitants it had disgorged that morning to go to work, or university, or whatever else they did with their days. She knocked again.

'I could get us inside, if you want?' said Hellendoorn, a surprising note of respectfulness in his voice. He was standing a few feet behind her, the skeleton key in his hand.

Napier glanced at him, feeling suddenly foolish. She stepped away from the door, imagining the apartment beyond, the way it had been five years ago; perhaps messy, clothes strewn across the sofa and the bedroom from when Katrin had been packing for her trip. Or perhaps meticulously tidy, everything carefully organised and laid out, minimalist and clutter-free.

She realised she still didn't know Katrin at all.

'No... that's okay. Let's go and try the suitcase again.'

In the end they managed to beat Wim's best time by a couple

of seconds, but couldn't get close to completing the round trip inside the time limit.

'So are you... satisfied... Hargreaves didn't... do it?' Hellendoorn asked midway through their fourth attempt. They were back in apartment 1211, the detective gasping for breath as he leaned against the wall.

She nodded, similarly exhausted. After she'd recovered, she told him about her meeting with Chikezie and Wu, and the name they had given her.

'Did you ever hear of a work colleague named Lukas Serafinowicz?'

'He was her number-one fan, right?' Once again, the detective's memory of the case proved exhaustive.

'That's what Wu says. That Serafinowicz was always asking her out for drinks, that sort of thing. Wu thinks that's who invited her to the party.'

Hellendoorn frowned. 'Her dad told me about Serafinowicz. He said he made some pretty inappropriate posts on her Facebook page – before she disappeared, I mean. So Gunnar asked me to investigate him specifically. But I remember the kid having an alibi for that night... so it would be *very* interesting if she went to the party with him, because it would mean he lied to me. You're thinking perhaps he tried it on with her, she said no, it got out of hand?'

'Maybe. But that's not what my mystery informant says.'

He blinked, looking baffled. 'Who?'

'That's my *other* new lead. I got a message on the Facebook page. Definitely a fake account, and they haven't replied to my messages back to them, but it's from someone saying they were at the party. They say they saw her leave in a white van, with an eye on the side.'

For just a moment, Hellendoorn's face seemed to transform. The jaded, cynical air that he wrapped around himself like a cloak was suddenly dispelled, the detective's eyes widening in childlike excitement. Then he collected himself, the mask restored.

'Probably just a crank. Is there a way you can trace them?'

'You know, I hadn't even considered that.' She thought about Isaac, whose computer skills had always seemed like alchemy to her. 'And I know just the man to ask.'

19

PODCAST EPISODE 8:

THE PARTY

Since our last episode, I've unearthed some more information. If it feels like the jigsaw pieces are coming so fast that you can't possibly put them all together, that makes two of us.

I told Wim Hellendoorn, the private investigator, about L, the work colleague of Katrin's that her friend Henry thinks might have invited her to the party. Henry also said that L was constantly pestering Katrin to go out on a date with him. Hellendoorn corroborated this story, and told me that Katrin's father even asked him specifically to investigate L after the man made some inappropriate Facebook posts on Katrin's page before she went missing.

That makes L another suspect. We've tried to get in touch with him, but he has since left Triton Homes and closed his Facebook account, and we haven't been able to track him down. I'm keeping his identity a secret for now in case he wants to make contact with the show, to clear his name; L, if you're listening, you'll know who you are. We would love to talk to you about that night, and what you remember – and why you gave Wim Hellendoorn a different story.

Meanwhile, we still have the Facebook post from our

mysterious informant, which suggests something completely different: that Katrin left the party in the Coughing Man's van. While I can't believe she would willingly climb into his vehicle, maybe something else happened – like perhaps she was drunk, or even drugged.

The post was made by what appears to be a fake Facebook account; as well as being named after the writer of *Alice's Adventures in Wonderland*, the profile picture depicts a young white man in a suit and tie, and the account is locked so you can't see who its friends are. So far, Lewis Carroll hasn't responded to any of my friend requests or messages; please, if you're listening, I implore you to get in touch with the show so we can find out more about this lead.

All of these clues and contradictions are starting to blow my mind. But it makes me more convinced than ever that the party at Tony Weaver's flat is the key to this thing. That's why, in today's episode, I want to recap everything we've learned to date, to see if we can shake loose any more information.

Fact one: We've now been told by three separate people that they remember seeing Katrin at Tony's flat that night: Jamal Habib, her personal trainer; Henry Wu, her friend from work; and Tony himself. So it seems almost irrefutable that she went to Hannibal Heights after arriving home from Iceland.

However, it should be noted that there are no records of another Ryde journey from her address that evening – so how did she get there? It's unlikely she walked the four miles to Meadowvale from Elephant and Castle in the middle of the night, and there are no public transport connections at that time. But if the decision was an impulsive one, she could have simply hailed a cab, or perhaps even arranged to be picked up by somebody.

Fact two: She talked to her friends about a mysterious man she was involved with, someone she called 'Mr Wolf'. Tony

Weaver also remembers her talking to him at the party about an older man who had hurt her somehow. Her friends think it was maybe one of the senior executives from Triton Homes.

Fact three: She was possibly invited to the party by L, a colleague who was a similar age to Katrin and was apparently very keen on her. Wim Hellendoorn was even asked by Katrin's father to investigate this man, specifically because of some posts he made on her Facebook page, but L had an alibi for the night in question – which means he quite possibly lied to Wim. It is worth noting, though, that the posts were made before she disappeared, so if Katrin was truly offended by L's comments, it seems unlikely that she would agree to go to a party with him.

Fact four: Jamal Habib, a personal trainer who Katrin had trained with at the gym and grown close to, was also at the party. He doesn't remember much about Katrin that night, as his attention was focused on his date for the evening. The fact that he was the person who told me about the party in the first place makes it unlikely that he is a serious suspect.

Fact five: Her friend Henry Wu also attended the party, but doesn't remember much, and claims he left because he was too drunk. He doesn't remember where Katrin went.

Fact six: A mystery contact on our Facebook page has told me they saw Katrin leaving in a van that matched the description of the one owned by the Coughing Man. Wim believes the van might have belonged to an operative from Focus Security Solutions, whose logo matches the description of an evil eye symbol on its side.

Wow. There's a lot to unpick here. I decided to start by going back to Hannibal Heights, for another meeting with Tony.

But first, I have something to explain. As I mentioned in a previous episode, and for reasons that at times make me doubt my own sanity, I've decided to participate in the same charity boxing event that Katrin did in the year before her disappearance. I'm signed up with the same promotion, training with the same coach, fighting at the same venue. As you may remember from my first meeting with Tony, he owns the promotion company. I don't think this gives me a conflict of interest – although, after being mercilessly beaten up for the last seven weeks of training, I'd be very happy at this point for an excuse not to fight – but I wanted to let you know. To be very clear, I don't want this story to be about me; but equally I don't want to be anything other than completely transparent.

This explains why, when I next met Tony, he asked, 'how's your training going?'

We were in the museum on the ground floor of the building, and never had The Animal House seemed more deserving of its nickname. Surrounding us were all manner of stuffed creatures: foxes, ocelots, eagles, even a walrus, all peering out from glass cases with something expectant in their eyes, as though waiting for someone to utter the magic word that would reanimate them all. The famous polar bear takes centre stage, facing off against the walrus in a dramatic attacking stance, lips peeled back in a terrifying snarl. I feel like I've walked into some bizarre, freeze-framed Attenborough documentary.

'I'm not dead yet, so okay I suppose. Can I ask why you won't let us use your real voice? No pressure – just curious.'

'Call it paranoia. I have a murky past.'

'I want to ask you about the party.'

'I've already told you what I remember.'

Even more grotesque were the specimens preserved in jars, their pickled bodies bleached a disturbing white. Rabbits, lizards, pigeons and monkeys surrounded us, all staring outwards with the horror and surprise of death etched into their shrivelled faces.

'I just want to check some facts. Like who attended. I've managed to find some others who claim they were there and that they saw Katrin, so it's very important that I figure out where she went afterwards. It could be critical to finding out what happened to her. So please – I need your help.'

Tony gave no outward sign of agreement, and instead started to wander around the exhibits, peering into each cabinet in turn. He paused for a while in front of a fruit bat, pinned upright with its wings spread wide apart. One of them was still covered by its black, leathery membrane, like a vampire's cloak thrown dramatically open. The other been stripped down to the bone to showcase its complex, oddly beautiful skeletal structure. The creature's head was propped upwards, wearing a confused but happy expression, like a dog.

'Can I show you some photographs?'

I'd prepared a sheet with some of the faces of the people I've met. Some of them were allegedly at his party, while some weren't. Others were complete red herrings, like a photo of my friend Isaac, who is appearing in this episode as Tony's vocal stand-in once again. I wanted to see if Tony picked out the right ones.

'Be my guest.'

I handed him the sheet of A4, which had twelve pictures on it.

'That's Katrin.'

He pointed at the first picture, which showed a blonde girl with a small, slender face, tapering almost to a point at her chin. She had the sort of delicate features that people call 'elfin'.

'That's right.'

'Pretty girl, wasn't she?'

'And still is, hopefully – we don't know if she's still alive.'

He just nodded thoughtfully, and didn't reply. I asked him if he recognised any of the others, and he pointed at a picture of Jamal Habib. 'This lad is one of the gym trainers. I had him coaching my classes at one point, but he was too unreliable. Kept not turning up.'

Sorry Jamal. The truth sometimes hurts.

'Was he at the party?'

'Couldn't tell you.'

He pointed to the last face on the page.

'Hang on – that's you, isn't it?'

'You caught me – that's a trick one. It's actually my mum, when she was a lot younger.'

'Well, I can see where you get your looks from.'

I think his comment was intended to be kind rather than flirty, but I couldn't help but be unsettled by the flash of steel in his grin. I noticed the necklace still around his neck, its gruesome adornments hidden beneath his shirt.

'Any others?'

I was hoping he would pick out L, of whom I'd managed to obtain an old photo, but instead he surprised me by pointing at a photo in the central column.

'This bloke looks familiar. Maybe he turned up at one point, late into it. I was like, "What's this old geezer doing in my flat?" Cramping my style, if you know what I mean. I can't tell you his name right now. But he was an executive at Triton Homes, where Katrin worked. They built this building.'

'A big dog, eh? Could he have been there to pick up Katrin?'

Tony had stopped in front of a marine exhibit. Eels, bass and salmon were displayed in all their silvery glory, as well as some more peculiar animals, like jellyfish and even a baby octopus. But Tony's attention was captured by the cabinet's centrepiece, a ten-foot-long mako shark. He bent to examine its head, peering into the glassy black orbs of its eyes, at the curved spines of its teeth.

'Sorry. I can't tell you if he was at the party, but I've definitely seen him before. None of the others ring a bell.'

'Can you remember if he was there with Katrin?'

'Nope. All I know is, it's never a good idea to mess with powerful creatures.'

He turned to flash me that grin again, his teeth the same colour as the shark's glistening skin.

Once again, I left a meeting with Tony Weaver with my head full of questions, and feeling a little shaken, for reasons I can't quite explain.

20

Isaac had insisted that they take a walk together 'somewhere peaceful', to help Napier unwind from the stresses of the case, and the demands of her training. She had expected the new manga exhibition at the British Museum or something similarly geeky, but he had surprised her by taking her to Kew Gardens.

She was by no means an enthusiastic horticulturalist (or an amateur gardener, or even someone who had owned a pot plant for over a decade), but as they strolled along Princess Walk she was mesmerised by the plants and their mid-November finery. The deciduous trees were wrapped in mantles of red, auburn, ochre and yellow, interspersed with evergreens that seemed to eye their resplendent cousins with envy.

But her thoughts were grim, as perhaps they had always been. Deep scarlet hues became the crimson of dried blood; orange reminded her Jamil's Halloween pumpkins, grinning evilly; yellows were the colour of old, dried bones. They were heading towards the Great Pagoda, and the structure jutting upwards from amongst the leafy canopy looked to Napier like a warlock's tower.

A deep thrum of pain speared her side, and she stopped, wincing as she clamped a hand to her bandaged ribs.

'Are you okay?' Isaac asked, his concerned cry jarring against the silent backdrop. There weren't many people in the gardens, and those that were there seemed hushed and reverent, as though a loud voice might rupture the place's melancholic beauty.

'It's nothing,' she replied.

'You know, no one will think any less of you if you drop out.'

'I'm not a *quitter*,' she barked, then felt guilty for the sudden venom in her words. 'I'm sorry, Isaac. Thank you for caring about me. I just... like to see things through, you know?'

He nodded dumbly, his expression like that of a scolded child.

Guilt gnawed at her, adding to the pain radiating from her bruised body. 'It's not just that,' she continued. 'It's addictive. I'm physically fitter than I've ever been right now, and I feel more confident. The other night we sparred against other fighters from the same event, and I held my own, and it was *good*.'

'I suppose I just don't understand, that's all,' Isaac replied with a frown. 'If I'm honest, it seems a little... beneath you. You're intelligent, talented, creative; I didn't expect you to get kicks out of punching people in the face.'

She was surprised at how much his words stung, and felt anger stir inside her once again. 'You aren't listening. Imagine walking around, for your entire life, as a *prey animal*. Every time a man looks at you, in a quiet street, alone in a train carriage, in a nightclub, a part of your brain starts screaming at you that you're going to get raped, mugged, murdered. Well now, for the first time, I feel like I can look them back in the eye and say, "Just try it – I'll rip your fucking head off."'

She glanced around, suddenly embarrassed, wondering if

anyone had overheard her outburst. A squirrel scurried across the path in front of them as though terrified of her.

'I'm sorry, Elaine. I didn't mean to offend you. I get it. I should be more supportive.' He smiled apologetically, extending his elbow.

She looped her arm through it; a tiny peace offering, a reset button. But she couldn't help thinking, *Do you though? Does any man really 'get it'?*

A few minutes later, the ominous gathering of clouds overhead disgorged a sudden and unforecast deluge of rain, so they changed direction and headed towards the shelter of the tropical greenhouse. Inside, surrounded by lofty palm trees and hot, cloying air, Napier felt as though she'd been transported to another world altogether, somewhere ancient and hostile. Some of the cycads predated the dinosaurs, and the plants seemed to lean down to peer at her as she walked amongst them, as though she was an unwanted, pinkish intruder.

They reminded her of the flowers in *Alice in Wonderland*.

'It feels like another planet,' she said, the temperature forcing her to take off her jacket.

'It *is* weird,' Isaac replied, looking around at the colossal leaves and gaudy flowers. 'Like a rainforest without any animals.'

'Do they have Venus flytraps?'

'I've been snapped at enough today, thanks.'

'Ouch.'

'Sorry. You know me, I can't resist a good burn.' He grinned, and she grinned back, and it felt as though all the accumulated tension had been melted away by the heat.

'By the way, I'm halfway through editing the Tony Weaver episode,' he continued. 'That was a great bit, when he was looking at the shark, talking about "powerful creatures". What a cheeseball.'

'I bet you enjoyed recording that line.'

'Yeah, but I'm worried I sound a bit over the top. I wish he'd let us use his real voice.'

'Just make sure I don't mention Horowitz's name. We're on thin ice, because we've already said that Katrin worked for Triton Homes. We can't make any direct accusations against him without more information.'

Blake Horowitz had been the director of the Hannibal Heights project. There had been other Triton executives on her photo sheet, but Weaver had recognised only him. There were a number of possible explanations for this, of course – Weaver might be misremembering someone else, or have met the executive at a different social event, given that he had bought an apartment in Triton's flagship development. It could even be a deliberate misdirection.

But there was something about that photo, of a successful businessman who had since left Triton Homes to take over as the regional CEO at a rival developer, that made Napier's skin crawl. Those beady eyes seemed to hide deep channels of ambition, even ruthlessness. His smile seemed entirely without warmth, an instrument to be deployed when required, like that of a politician.

Or a wolf.

'I noticed you didn't ask Weaver about Martina?' Isaac's question drew her out of her thoughts.

'No... I should talk to her first. I don't want to mention her on the podcast if I can avoid it. I think she's quite a private person.'

'Who likes fighting in a cage in front of hundreds of people?'

'You know what I mean. It's different.'

'So what are you thinking for the next show?'

'Hellendoorn is trying to track down Hargreaves, the Ryde driver, but I'm not sure I could stand recording another "sad" episode. I'd rather get hold of L – sorry, I mean Lukas

Serafinowicz. God, I'm starting to forget when I can and can't use real names!'

'Could Hellendoorn help you find him, too?'

'I already asked him. I'm beginning to feel like I'm taking advantage of the poor man.'

'Like you do with me, you mean?'

'Yes, but you're *obliged* to help, because you're my friend.'

'Just remember you owe me a favour, Napes. I won't forget this. I'm like an elephant.'

'Grey-skinned and slow?'

He deployed his most withering of looks, and she laughed.

'Speaking of free detective work, I'm not having much luck tracking down your Lewis Carroll. Facebook will only help if it's an impostor account, as in someone pretending to be someone else; but it isn't an impostor account, or at least I can't prove it is, which means they won't tell me who set it up, because of data protection. I even tried using reverse image search software on the profile picture so I could show Facebook that it's been stolen from another site – but I can't find the photo anywhere else online.'

'So maybe that's his real face?'

'Then why the secrecy? If he's happy to show his face, why the locked account and the radio silence?'

'Perhaps he's just a nutter.'

Isaac scratched his chin thoughtfully. Normally clean-shaven, he seemed to be experimenting with designer stubble, which Napier thought looked good on him.

'I could speak to him directly, through the show,' she mused. 'He obviously wants my attention – perhaps I could say I have a new policy of completely ignoring posts of that type, unless they contact me directly with compelling information.'

Isaac frowned. 'I don't know; it seems dangerous, somehow.

And what if that means we suddenly get loads of other weirdos writing in?'

'Maybe he's not a weirdo. Maybe he's telling the truth.'

'It might not even really be a "he".'

Napier grimaced in frustration, then she heard her phone vibrating in her jacket pocket, and made an apologetic gesture as she took it out. It was an unknown mobile number.

'This is Elaine Napier,' she answered, the same greeting she had used for years as a journalist, where answering mysterious calls from unknown numbers had been commonplace.

'This is DI Demetriou. We spoke a few weeks ago about your... broadcast.'

Napier's eyes widened. She signalled frantically to Isaac, calling him over to press his ear against hers, the phone sandwiched between them.

'Yes, I remember. How can I help you, detective?'

'I need you to kill it.'

Napier blinked. 'I'm sorry?'

'The podcast. It needs to stop. You're damaging the integrity of an ongoing investigation.'

Isaac looked at her, alarm in his face.

'Ongoing, is it?' Napier replied acidly. 'Doesn't seem that way to me.'

'This is not a discussion.'

Napier took a deep breath.

'I'm afraid that I have no intention of stopping, detective. There is no legal impediment to me reporting on a cold case of this nature – in fact, there are a number of other podcasts that provide the precedent. Some of them have helped the police to solve serious crimes. So maybe you should try working with me, instead of trying to shut me up.'

Demetriou continued, undeterred. 'We're getting complaints, phone calls, loads of cranks coming out of the woodwork because of you. I could charge you for wasting police time.'

'Have you even looked into the leads I've unearthed? The party, the work colleagues–'

'I'll stop you there, Miss Napier. As I've already said, I'm not calling to argue with you. I'm calling to instruct you, formally, to stop making your programme.'

Napier felt the rage coiling inside her once again, like a serpent shifting in her belly. 'And I'm telling you to go and fuck yourself. You and your team have completely failed Katrin. The case was buried in an archive somewhere until we started this thing. So you morons should be thanking me for doing your jobs for you.'

She ended the call, her breathing heavy, heart like a jackhammer in her chest. A couple of people had stopped to stare at her, but looked away as she caught their eye, suddenly fascinated by the fronds of some nearby ferns.

At her side, Isaac had started to applaud.

21

PODCAST EPISODE 9:

THE COUGHING MAN

Once again, I'd like to thank all of our listeners for their support, encouragement and interaction since we started this show. We've received many more messages and reviews than I could ever have hoped for, and I apologise to anyone that we haven't gotten around to responding to yet – the truth is that we're a team of two, and we're working as hard as we can to follow up on every lead. Contact details will follow at the end of the episode if you want to get in touch with us; we want to hear your thoughts and theories, however outlandish, because one of them might just be the breakthrough we need to solve this case.

One subject that crops up often on our discussion forum is the identity of the white van driver. Marcus Dobson, Katrin's boyfriend at the time of her disappearance, is convinced that this man was her abductor. And private investigator Wim Hellendoorn – himself another very popular figure with our listeners – believed strongly enough in this theory to interview over a dozen people.

In today's episode, Wim is joining me to discuss everything we know about the so-called Coughing Man.

'The first thing I did was to confirm the phone call from Katrin to Marcus.'

Wim had a thick, yellowing case file open on his desk, but I felt as though this was just for effect; he seems to have every scrap of information about the case committed to his encyclopaedic memory.

'Katrin's phone disappeared with her, but I checked Marcus's, and the call did come through from her device at just after midnight. That doesn't mean the Coughing Man exists, of course.'

'Is there any way to get a recording of the call, Wim? From the phone company, or something?'

'No. All I can say is the call lasted three minutes, which fits the timing of her finishing the call to Marcus, then ordering a Ryde from her phone straight afterwards, and being picked up by John H at twenty past.'

'So we can't prove that Marcus didn't just invent the Coughing Man?'

'That's correct. But we've both interviewed the kid, and we believe him, right? And you've got to remember that if he's lying about this, then that probably makes him her abductor... but the police grilled him for days, and didn't turn up anything. Then I grilled him again. By the end he probably felt like a pork chop.'

Every time a conversation turns to any of the suspects, my brain immediately screams at me that *of course it's him, it's so obvious, he's getting away with murder*.

Then I remember poor Marcus, sitting in his flat, consumed with grief and anger.

And that's the problem with a case like this. Everyone seems guilty when you look at them from one angle, and innocent from another. Like a hall of mirrors.

'Wim, assuming his story is true, what does that tell us about the Coughing Man?'

'Quite a lot, actually. I pushed Marcus hard to remember as much detail as he could, and in the end I was able to write what I think is a decent transcript of the conversation he had with Katrin.'

'Can you read it out?'

'Er, yes, okay.'

He flipped through the swollen file, which looked as though it was bursting at the seams with loose papers, Post-it notes and Polaroid photographs. Most of the contents were written in Hellendoorn's sloping scrawl, with other comments and annotations in the margins in differently coloured inks. I thought of my own case notes at home, copious but nothing compared to that bulging tome, and realised just how much time and effort Hellendoorn had put into the case over the years, despite never being paid.

I'd have asked to borrow it but, of course, it's all in Dutch.

'I've got to stress that this is just an approximation of what was said; almost like an artist's impression of a face, you know? Ah, here it is.'

He reached into his top pocket and pulled out a pair of reading glasses, squinting as he perched them on the end of his nose. For a moment the grizzled detective was replaced by a bookish, sweet-looking old man. Then he cleared his throat noisily, and I couldn't help but grimace as he spat into his wastepaper bin.

'Better out than in. Okay, yes, so it starts with Marcus picking up the phone.'

I've re-recorded the next section with me filling in Katrin's parts, so it's easier for you to tell who's speaking.

'Hi! Did you finally make it?'

'Yeah, I've just got through security – can you come and pick me up?'

'I thought you were getting the train?'

'I've missed the last one 'cos of the stupid delay.'

'Oh no! Sweetie, I can't – my car's in the garage, remember?'

'Oh. I forgot. Shit. Can't you get a taxi to come and get me?'

'Why don't you just get a taxi straight here?'

'Hmph... no, I just want my own bed. It was such a terrible flight.'

'You mean the delay?'

'Not just that. There was this fucking guy sat next to me, talking to me all the way, even when I put my headphones in. You know, I think he's still watching me.'

'What? What do you mean, watching you?'

'He kept telling me about his van, offering to give me a lift home after the flight. And now it's parked right near me, just waiting there.'

'How do you know it's his van?'

'Well, I don't. But it's got a weird logo on the side, like an evil eye symbol, and it's all rusted and battered. It kind of reminds me of him. And why is it just sitting there?'

'Who was this bloke?'

'I don't know, I didn't ask him his name. He kept talking even when I put my headphones in. He was just really gross, you know, overweight and smelly, wearing these pants and a shirt that were about two sizes too small and covered in stains. His beard was like... ohh who is it, with bits of old food in it, so he can have a snack whenever he wants one?'

'I don't know what you're on about.'

'Mr Twit! You remember? The Roald Dahl book I made you read? *And* he kept coughing and sneezing, breathing all over me when he talked. I'm worried I've caught something.'

'He probably just fancied you. 'Cos you're so pwettyyy...'

Hellendoorn looked so uncomfortable as he pronounced this word that he almost had me in hysterics.

'Stop it, Marcus, it's not funny – I want you to come and get me.'

'Just get a Ryde here. I'll have a hot water bottle and loads of cuddles waiting for you. I want to see you.'

'Forget it. I'll just go home. I've got to be up early for bloody work. I'll see you tomorrow night.'

'I'm really sorry about the car, sweetie. You know I'd be there if I could.'

'It's fine.'

'Please just come here? I've missed you.'

'Bye, Marcus.'

'Okay. Bye then.'

And that was the last thing Dobson ever said to her. So innocuous, so empty. Despite its inevitability, death takes us all by surprise; we never remember to say 'I love you' as if it's for the last time.

'So once you were convinced Marcus was telling the truth, you turned your attention to trying to track down the van.'

'Yes. The insignia should have made it easy to find.'

The evil eye symbol is something of a contradiction. To give someone 'the evil eye' is to wish misfortune upon them while they are unaware, almost like a curse. However, the symbol itself, also referred to as the evil eye, is a depiction of a staring eye that is supposed to ward off these sorts of ill wishes. The idea appears across many religions, countries and cultures, and is referenced as far back as the ancient Greeks. Talismans to protect against the evil eye are common, including the Turkish hamsa (an eye in the centre of a warding hand), a blue or turquoise bead worn around the neck in Assyrian cultures, or small pieces of black cloth on the bumpers of public transport vehicles in Pakistan.

The evil eye even appears in the very first chapter of Bram Stoker's *Dracula*, when Jonathan Harker is making his trip to

Eastern Europe to conclude a property transaction with the infamous Count.

'...the crowd round the inn door, which had by this time swelled to a considerable size, all made the sign of the cross and pointed two fingers towards me. With some difficulty I got a fellow-passenger to tell me what they meant; he would not answer at first, but on learning that I was English he explained that it was a charm or guard against the evil eye.'

Of course, the 'evil eye' could have simply been Katrin's own interpretation of an image that in fact had a completely different meaning. One connotation of a staring eye is watchfulness, or surveillance, which is why the symbol would make complete sense for a security company. Wim's diligent investigation had unearthed a company called Focus Security Solutions, based in Woking, which traded between 2001 and 2017 before being bought out by a larger rival.

'How many drivers did you interview?'

'They were only a small company. I met the owner and his eight drivers. All men. The vans were kept at a depot when they weren't in use, and I checked their security footage for the night she disappeared: only two vans were out on jobs. But I met with all the drivers anyway.'

'Did any other employees have access to the vans?'

'The only other employee was the owner's wife; she manned the phones, maintained their accounts, basically did all their admin while her husband was out trying to win contracts.'

'And you don't think any of the drivers could be the Coughing Man?'

Wim shook his head. 'The two drivers who were out in the vans didn't match the description at all – one was in his early twenties and of very slim build, and the other was a bodybuilder.'

'What about the others?'

JON RICHTER

'There were a couple of guys who might have fit the bill if they grew a beard and didn't change clothes for a week, but the more important point is that they were all working that week – so none of them could have been on a flight back from Iceland.'

I took their names from Wim all the same, but the CCTV evidence, and the alibis, seem pretty watertight. I could sense Wim's frustration even as he retold the story.

'You really wanted it to be them, didn't you?'

'I even checked the two vans myself, tried to persuade the police to screen them for her DNA. But sometimes you can get too hung up on something. The truth was, neither of the vans was battered or rusty, like Katrin described it – they were both pretty much like new.'

'So what was next?'

'I became obsessed with that vehicle. At one point I even started just driving around, hoping to find a rusted van with an eye painted on the side.'

I was reminded of Marcus, once again. I imagined the two of them, Dobson and Hellendoorn, prowling the streets, both pursuing the same obsession, from very different perspectives.

'But the truth is, if it was used in a crime, it was probably repainted or dumped afterwards. Meanwhile, I moved on to the passengers.'

There were 188 people on the CrystalAir flight from Reykjavik to Gatwick that night. It was a Boeing 757-200, with a capacity of 224, and the two seats next to Katrin should have been unoccupied.

'I managed to get hold of a complete manifest. Exactly half of the passengers were female, and another eighteen were children, so that leaves seventy-six people who could have been the Coughing Man.'

'Assuming he exists.'

'Assuming he exists.'

'Do airlines give out passenger manifests?'

'Nope. So I probably shouldn't be telling you this.'

'Did they give you any other information?'

'This was the most I could get my hands on. It's very difficult to trace seventy-six people when all you have is a name.'

Wim showed me the list, with the women and children scribbled out in red pen. Wim had also crossed off the names of five men he's managed to track down so far, and ruled out, leaving just seventy-one names to go. It's so frustrating – just like looking at the numbers in the lottery, not knowing which ones are going to come up that weekend.

'Of the people I've found, no one remembers seeing a someone matching the Coughing Man's description, and no one remembers seeing Katrin either.'

This is where our listeners might be able to help. I can't broadcast the names for reasons of confidentiality, but if you were on that flight, or if you know someone who was, please get in touch. I've put the exact time, flight number and other details in the show notes.

I should also mention our mysterious Facebook contact, Lewis Carroll, who messaged us a couple of weeks ago to tell us they had seen Katrin climbing into a van with 'an eye on the side' after the party on the night she went missing. If this is true, it is absolutely vital information – but we still haven't heard from Lewis since that message.

I'm sure this person is listening to the show. Please, I urge you to get in touch with us, even if your post was just a prank; I promise there will be no consequences.

We just want the truth.

Wim told me the other angles he's pursued over the years, such as trying to get hold of airport CCTV footage of the long-stay car park, or trying to discuss the Coughing Man directly with the police detectives investigating the case. All have proved fruitless.

'I know it's a cliché, but it really does feel like the earth just swallowed her up.'

I only said it in passing, but Wim couldn't have looked more disgusted.

'No, Elaine. The earth didn't take her at all; if you start saying things like that then you've already given up. The earth only takes us when we die. Katrin wasn't ready to die. The only thing that swallowed up that girl was the son of a bitch driving that white van.'

22

TRANSCRIPT OF COUNSELLING SESSION WITH ELAINE NAPIER, 1994

Doctor Julian Martin: Why do you think you're here today, Elaine?

Elaine: Because my teachers hate me.

Julian: Why do you think they hate you?

Elaine: …

Julian: What exactly did you do?

Elaine: …

Julian: Your mother tells me you stabbed someone with a compass this week.

Elaine: She's not my mother.

Julian: Why do you say that?

Elaine: It was his fault anyway. He said something nasty about Sam. If the teachers did anything about it, I wouldn't keep hurting people, would I?

Julian: Sam's your sister, who disappeared?

Elaine: Is that what it says in your little notebook?

Julian: You seem very hostile, Elaine. I'm just here to help you.

Elaine: Well it would help me if we could get a move on. I've got homework to do.

Julian: Do you work hard at school?

Elaine: <Laughs>

Julian: It seems like your sister's disappearance affected you a great deal.

Elaine: No shit, Sherlock.

Julian: What do you think happened to her?

Elaine: I think she's dead.

Julian: Why do you believe that?

Elaine: Because she realised how shit this life really is.

Julian: You mean you think she killed herself?

Elaine: <Inaudible>

Julian: Sorry Elaine, I can't hear you.

Elaine: I said it's better than the alternative.

Julian: Why is it better?

Elaine: 'Cos that would mean some man got her.

Julian: How would that make you feel?

Elaine: …

Julian: Please Elaine, it would be much easier for me to help you if you could open up a little.

Elaine: All right then. Do you have children, doctor?

Julian: I do.

Elaine: Boys or girls?

Julian: A son, Oliver, and a daughter, Kate.

Elaine: Imagine if some horrible scumbag

kidnapped Kate, then tortured and raped her, and then hid her body in the woods somewhere. Then imagine that no one could find her, for two years. Her bones were just lying there, slowly rotting away, chewed and pulled apart by foxes—

Julian: Okay, Elaine, that's enough.

Elaine: Well, then. Don't ask questions if you don't want to know the answers.

23

'Everything just feels completely stagnated,' Napier sighed. 'Horowitz won't speak to me, and neither will anyone connected to him – and I can't get any of the execs still at Triton Homes to talk either.'

'What about Serafinowicz, or the Ryde driver? Has Hellendoorn been able to get hold of them?'

'He just says "sometimes these things take time" and gives me that fucking shrug, like he's a Buddhist master of the art of patience.'

'Well I don't mean to add to your woes, Elaine, but the next episode is due on Wednesday, so unless you get me something tomorrow then it's not going to be ready in time.'

'I know, I know. Look, I've got to go – I've just arrived at the gym, and Martina will tear strips off me if I'm late.'

'Normally I'd assume that was a metaphor, but in this case I'm not so sure. Er... have fun?'

'Ahhh shit, where's my gym pass?' But Isaac had already hung up, and she was left cursing into the phone held clamped between her cheek and shoulder while she fumbled in her bag for the membership card.

Week ten. A fortnight of training left. At the end of this week she'd find out who her opponent was. There were a few candidates, all of similar build and weight to her, and the prospect of having to fight some of them filled her with dread. But she wouldn't show them that, of course. Not tonight. They didn't know about the painkillers, the bandages, the fear that squirmed in her belly every time she clambered between the ropes.

The others had congregated around the ring, putting on their wraps, taking a final swig of water or a last glance at their phone. She surveyed the rest of the group: seven other women and nine men, meaning they would have to draft in an extra opponent to even the numbers on fight night. She realised that she hadn't bothered to forge real friendships with any of them. Most were younger than her, and taking the event extremely seriously, their expressions hard and demeanours surly before and after the sessions; but still, several had made an effort to say hello, to try to find out a little about her. She'd been polite but cold, her mind elsewhere, focusing on learning the techniques as best she could.

Every person in that group had a different reason for fighting. Some fought for a thrill, to force themselves far from their comfort zone. Some fought for charity, raising money through sponsorships and ticket sales. Some fought because of their high self-esteem, others because of a lack of it. But all of them seemed to be searching for something, a new facet to their lives that wasn't just work, or drinking, or dating.

What are you searching for, Elaine?

Except for Martina, she hadn't told any of them about the podcast. She'd kept them all at a distance, like a boxer using their jab to create separation, avoiding the dangers of building a relationship. It suddenly felt like a metaphor for her whole life.

As she glanced again around the ring at the assembled faces, she felt inexplicable resentment bubbling inside her.

'Okay, we're gonna warm up,' came Martina's voice. 'A few stretches, then some shadow boxing.'

After fifteen minutes they switched to sparring. There was no more teaching, no further tutorials on how to throw a perfect uppercut or block an incoming right hook. The best training now was simulated combat. Napier's turn soon came, the others watching from outside the ring as though the gym had transformed into an underground fight club.

What a strange situation, thought a part of Napier's brain as she circled her opponent. The other part of her brain, the animal part, the atavistic, fight-or-flight part, was staring into the other girl's eyes, trying to predict her opening move.

At least it wasn't Nicola, the firefighter and bodybuilding enthusiast, who at nearly six feet tall towered above the rest of the group. More than anyone else, she exuded the distinct impression that she'd signed up for the fight purely because she liked to hurt people.

This girl's name was Sophie: a short, stocky Australian with dark hair and determination in her face. Her mouth was twisted into a confident smirk as they circled each other, and perhaps a hint of something else: a hidden paranoia, a fear of embarrassment disguised behind her brash aggression.

A sparring session is supposed to be much lighter than a real bout; a practice round, where you test your ability to dodge, block, and land your punches. It wasn't about pummelling your opponent with full-power shots. But Napier saw, too late, the hostility in Sophie's eyes, realising just before her first blow landed that the girl was looking to make a point. Napier's head snapped backwards, the punch connecting cleanly with the centre of her face, like a dart into a bullseye.

Around her, the rest of the group gave a collective gasp.

She could hear Martina saying something, which might have been 'Sophie, take it easy, it's just sparring,' but her coach's voice sounded as though it was coming from somewhere far away. Napier's head felt submerged, as though weighted with rocks and tossed into a lake somewhere, her skull splintering beneath gallons of crushing water.

Then Sophie stepped forward, and Napier swung a huge haymaker in desperation, which her opponent deftly avoided. As the girl advanced again, Napier felt something crystallise inside her; the frustration of the case, her unresolved rage at her sacking from *The Chron*, her fury at all the people that gave her pitying glances when they found out she was single, childless and nearly forty years old.

Maybe I don't want children. Maybe I know what can happen to them.

She saw her mother's face, the sneer of disappointment that had tortured her teenage years, had followed everything she ever told the woman about her life, her dreams, her career, as inevitably as a punctuation mark.

You'll never amount to anything, Elaine.

Even after dementia had eroded her mother's mind, like stark cliffs sanded away by the ocean, that *look* had remained. A vestige of disapproval, haunting the dribbling husk of her mother's body like a spiteful ghost.

When I look at you, I can't help thinking God took the wrong daughter from me.

Then the face changed. Her mother's jowly features tightened, her mouth shrinking into a cold, uninterested sneer she had seen only once in the flesh, inside a courtroom, where she had stared at it from the public gallery.

You're a failure, Elaine. Your schoolteachers knew it, The Chronicle *knew it, and soon the rest of the world will know it.*

She had seen that face many times since, of course; in the

photo she had clipped from a newspaper, and in the images that
sometimes haunted her dreams.

Katrin's family – they'll know it.

The face grinned at her.

Like everyone else, you've let them down, too.

'Fuck *you!*'

The words seemed to burst out of her unconsciously, like
flies from their larval casing, as she rammed a nasty uppercut
into Sophie's ribs. She barely registered the surprise in the girl's
face, didn't notice the frown quickly transforming into pain,
then panic, as Napier followed up with two more uppercuts,
then a sort of jumping right cross that sent both her and her
opponent crashing to the floor.

Napier still felt as though she was underwater, but now the
waters were boiling and crimson, and seemed to churn with that
face, with *his* face.

I'm gone, but that didn't bring your sister back, did it?

She drove her fist into that hateful smirk.

*They never come back, Elaine. It's about time you learned to
accept it.*

'Shut up... shut up shut up shut up!'

She didn't stop raining blows onto that face until she felt
strong arms dragging her backwards. Bundled to the floor, she
blinked, confused, as she stared upwards into Martina's zircon-
blue eyes, the fighter pinning her down with an iron grip.

'Elaine! What the hell are you doing?'

The waters receded. The gym's harsh lighting was like the
light of the sun, shining suddenly into her face as she emerged,
breathless, gasping for air.

'I...' she began, then looked to the side. Sophie was being
helped to a sitting position, her face bruised and bloodied. She
shot Napier a look of unfiltered hatred as she struggled to her
feet. 'Fucking psycho!' she hissed.

Napier's mouth tried to form various words, settling eventually on 'I'm sorry'. She said it to no one, to everyone. To Sophie, to Martina, to herself, even to Katrin.

To Sam.

'Go home, and calm down,' Martina said severely. 'Don't come back to training this week unless you can keep a cool head.'

Napier climbed groggily to her feet, her head still vibrating like a struck bell. She felt the stares of the others on her – outraged, shocked – as she left the ring, and didn't make eye contact with any of them as she stuffed her things into her bag. She saw blood on her gloves, blood mixed with her saliva as she extracted her gum shield. The taste of blood in her mouth. The feel of hardened chunks of it congealing inside her swollen nose.

Then a shadow loomed over her, and she looked up into the face of Tony Weaver. For a moment she couldn't work out why he was there; he was like a hallucination, something vomited up from a bad dream. Then she remembered that this was his boot camp, and Martina was his woman. She stared at him dumbly, at the tattooed patterns crawling up his neck like some sort of spreading disease. He looked down impassively. Despite his short stature he seemed to tower above her, colossus-like. Then he slowly extended a hand to help her to her feet; she took it, feeling more afraid to refuse his offer than to accept it. He flashed her a metallic grin, and winked, before turning his attention back towards the ring.

Well done, he had meant. *I like what I see.*

She hurried out of the gym, feeling contaminated.

It wasn't until much later that she cried, after she had drunk most of the bottle of vodka she'd bought on the way home. At several points her hand had lingered over Isaac's number, a couple of times over Hellendoorn's. But what would she say to them?

Hi, sorry to bother you, but I just brutalised a girl during training and now I feel terrible, so I'm drinking myself into a stupor. How are things with you?

When the phone rang in her hand, she realised that she'd fallen asleep, where more faces had come to haunt her. Her eyes sagged closed once again even as she answered.

'Hmm?'

'Elaine, it's Isaac. You need to check your emails, right now.'

24

PODCAST EPISODE 10:

THE VIDEO

Yesterday we received another message from Lewis Carroll. It wasn't a Facebook post this time; instead, it was a direct email to the show's inbox. The sender address was 'murky_water@xmail.com', and the subject line was 'a gift from your friend lewis carroll', all in lower case.

There was no text in the email itself, just a single attachment. It turned out to be a short video clip, without sound, lasting just under four minutes. It looks like CCTV footage, with a time and date stamp showing that it was recorded on the night of Katrin's disappearance, at 4.06am.

The footage is from inside a lift, with the camera in a corner facing diagonally downwards towards the control buttons. The doors are closed, but after a few seconds they slide open, and someone gets inside. The picture quality is grainy, but you can tell it's Katrin. She's wearing denim jeans and a white blouse, but doesn't have anything on her feet, as though she has, perhaps, left somewhere in a hurry. This is reinforced by her behaviour: she presses herself against the wall, glancing back out through the doors repeatedly to check for whatever or whoever she is hiding from. She looks distressed, and a little spacey, as if she's maybe drunk or drugged, and forgets to press any buttons for about twenty seconds. Then she suddenly remembers, and hits lots of them in a frenzy, lighting up the keypad. If you look closely, you can see that one of the buttons is the 'hold' button, which is probably why the lift doesn't go anywhere. This only intensifies her panic, and she continues mashing buttons and peeking back out into the corridor. Her expression as she does this is really troubling, her eyes wide and frightened, terrified even.

After a couple of minutes of trying to get the lift to move, she takes another look down the corridor, and then holds up her hands, stepping out of the lift. She talks to someone for maybe another minute – she's slightly out of shot at this point, but you can see her hands making big gestures while she talks, just like Henry Wu told me was her habit. She seems to be trying to reason with this person, flitting between trying to calm them down and getting annoyed herself.

Whoever she's talking to is off to the right, out of shot.

After a while Katrin stops, staring and listening, presumably because the other person is saying something. At one point she shakes her head firmly. Then she suddenly turns and runs away. The terror in her face in those final moments, and the speed with which she spins to flee, suggests that whoever she was talking to lunged suddenly towards her, perhaps starting to give chase. Within moments they would have crossed the gap in the corridor that is visible through the open lift doors, and we would see them on the video clip. And yet, so tantalisingly close to showing us the face of her mysterious assailant, the footage cuts off, right there.

Less than a second away from revealing the identity of Katrin's possible abductor.

Whoever Lewis Carroll is, I have no idea how he or she has obtained this footage. I also have no idea why they're sending us these clues and titbits. But I'm more convinced now than ever that, whoever they are, they are implicated somehow. Perhaps this is even some twisted form of a confession.

We know that Katrin attended a party at Hannibal Heights the night she disappeared, and the footage could certainly be from the same building; the corridor depicted through the lift doors is dark and hard to identify. I contacted the facilities manager to ask about the footage; this is a transcript of my – brief – conversation with him.

'Hello? This is Elaine Napier with *The Frozen Files* podcast. I'm trying to identify the source of some CCTV footage I've been sent.'

'They told me you'd call.'

'Sorry?'

'The police. They came to go through the archives, and they said that if anyone from a podcast called, I wasn't supposed to speak to them.'

'But, wait, you mean they–'

'Sorry, but I don't want to get in any trouble.'

And with that he hung up.

Does this mean that someone inside the police force has leaked the footage to us? Why on earth would they do that? I've shared the email with the police of course, but the detective in charge of the case refuses to discuss anything with me, so once again I'm left in the dark, clutching at straws. I feel certain that there's more to the video, another version where we see who is chasing Katrin, who made her so frightened that she tore off down the hallway in bare feet at 4 o'clock in the morning. Perhaps the police already have this information. Perhaps an arrest will soon be made.

Meanwhile, I've pored over the footage countless times, trying to work out from her expression whether she knew the person, and if so how she knew them. Was it a stranger? A friend? A jealous partner?

I've shared a link to the video in the show notes, so as always, I'm really keen to hear your ideas and theories.

As for Lewis Carroll, I'm going to address them directly. I've stopped hoping that you'll contact us to explain your actions. I don't understand what you want. Perhaps you want me to beg for your help; to grovel, here on the air, to make you feel important? If this is some sick power fantasy, then just remember that these are real lives you're toying with. Katrin's parents need to know what happened to their daughter. *I* need to know.

If you won't speak to me, then for God's sake at least send me the rest of the tape.

25

Hellendoorn placed the steaming mugs on the tabletop, his hands shaking slightly. Like him, like his office, like his car, the stained cups looked old and well-used.

'Cheers,' Napier and Isaac said simultaneously. Hellendoorn lowered his sizeable bulk into the (old, well-used) chair opposite them, extracting the (old, well-used) bottle of genever from the desk and pouring himself a generous slug.

'I watched the video,' the detective said after draining his glass in a single gulp. 'It's undoubtedly her. We need to find this Lewis Carroll.'

'Why do you think he's sending us this stuff?' Isaac asked, grimacing as he took a slurp of the coffee.

'Or she,' Napier added.

Hellendoorn gave one of his now-infamous shrugs. 'If it's Katrin's abductor, it doesn't make any sense. Why give us clues and information that might help us track them down? So perhaps it's someone who *wants* us to find out the truth, but is too afraid to go directly to the police.'

'Which means they know the truth themselves,' mused Napier, sipping from her own cup. The brew was thick and strong, but not as bad as Isaac's reaction had suggested. Or perhaps she was just too far down the road of caffeine addiction to care.

'Or they *think* they know,' added Isaac.

'And then we have the next mystery, which is how they actually *obtained* the footage,' Hellendoorn continued. 'Like you said, it could be someone inside the police investigation team.'

'It still makes no sense,' said Napier. 'If they're not happy with how Demetriou is running things, surely there are better ways to deal with it.'

'It could be Demetriou herself,' volunteered Isaac. 'Maybe her hands are tied, somehow. She can't follow up on the leads properly, or she doesn't have the resources, or whatever. So she's trying to get us to do the legwork for her.'

'Nah, I don't buy that. If she wants us to help her, she's got a funny way of showing it.'

'She'll be pretty pissed off when we broadcast the episode and she finds out we've got the video,' Isaac mused. 'Are we sure she doesn't have any legal power to shut us down?'

'As long as I'm not disclosing confidential information or prejudicing the outcome of a trial, she can't do anything to us,' replied Napier resolutely. She touched her nose, feeling it still swollen and tender from the sparring session; both Isaac and Hellendoorn had stared at it on first seeing her, but had thought better of commenting.

'The clothes Katrin was wearing, in the video,' Hellendoorn said as he poured himself another drink. 'We should confirm they were hers.'

Napier could picture them vividly. She'd watched the footage again and again, memorising every movement Katrin made, every exaggerated gesture or facial tic. Aside from the boxing video, it was the first time she had ever seen the girl in motion; as a living person with needs and fears and a beating heart, rather than just a tragic smile frozen in a photograph.

'I tried contacting Marcus, her boyfriend, to ask whether he recognised them,' replied Napier, eyes downcast.

'And?'

'He won't speak to me either. He thinks we're dragging Katrin's name through the mud.'

Her eyes were fixed on her hand, which was outstretched and resting on Hellendoorn's desk. The knuckles were scabbed from the boxing, the skin seeming stretched and thin and old. She felt a great, crushing wave of sadness sweep over her. Was Marcus Dobson right? Was she trashing an innocent young girl's reputation? And in the pursuit of what? Recognition? Fame? She certainly wasn't making any money.

Isaac seemed to sense her mood, and reached out to give her hand a gentle squeeze. Hellendoorn leaned back in his seat, emitting a loud creaking noise that could have come from the chair or from his ancient bones themselves. He interlaced his fingers behind his head, aiming a long exhalation up towards the ceiling where an archaic fan hung, motionless and dusty.

'I have some updates for you,' he said eventually. 'Lukas Serafinowicz is travelling. He's two months into a six-month round-the-world backpacking excursion, and only checks in infrequently with his parents in Leicester. I've asked them to get him to contact us, but don't hold your breath.'

'Where is he now?'

'Borneo, apparently.'

'Do you believe them?'

'He moved out of his last apartment two months ago and gave his parents' address for forwarded mail. It seems to stack up.'

'For fuck's sake,' Napier hissed. She realised her hand had curled unconsciously into a fist, and opened it again, feeling as though the limb belonged to someone else. 'Every lead turns out to be a dead end.'

'Don't speak too soon,' Hellendoorn replied, raising an eyebrow mischievously. 'I have two phone numbers for you. One is for John Hargreaves, the Ryde driver. He lives in Stevenage now, in and out of hostels and homeless shelters.'

'Shit. The poor guy.'

Hellendoorn nodded. 'The other might be more interesting. I spoke to Niamh Kennedy, and she's agreed to speak with you.'

Napier frowned. 'Who is Niamh Kennedy?'

Once again, that twinkle in Hellendoorn's dark-blue eyes, like something glinting at the bottom of a deep pool. 'She spent eleven years as Niamh Horowitz. She's Mr Wolf's ex-wife.'

26

PODCAST EPISODE 11:

THE PREDATORS

In the last few days of her life, Katrin seemed to be surrounded by men, and I can't help thinking of a shoal of piranhas circling their stricken prey. I've met some of them already, while others remain elusive. All were potentially at the party the night she disappeared, and any of them could be the person with whom she was arguing in the tantalising piece of CCTV footage we've obtained.

There's Tony Weaver, the boxing promoter, at whose apartment the party took place. He is adamant he didn't invite Katrin himself, but he does remember her being there.

There's the Coughing Man, of course; our mysterious online informant claims that he or she saw Katrin getting into his van at the end of the party, or at least into a vehicle matching that description.

There's L, the work colleague who might have invited her. We've ascertained that he's out of the country on a long backpacking holiday, but we're still very keen to speak with him, and to understand his memories of that evening.

Then there's Jamal, Katrin's personal trainer, and also Henry Wu, her friend, who were at the party too.

And finally there's Blake Horowitz. I've redacted his name in previous episodes, but now I've decided to go public, partly to encourage him to give me his side of the story. He was the project director during Hannibal Heights' design and construction, and Katrin's ultimate boss – and Tony Weaver claims he was also in attendance that night.

Yesterday I spoke on the phone with Niamh Kennedy, his ex-wife, who has allowed me to broadcast the recording of our conversation.

'Hello?'

'Hi Niamh. This is Elaine Napier from *The Frozen Files* podcast. I believe you spoke with my associate, Wim Hellendoorn?'

'Yes, that's right. He said you wanted to speak to me about Blake.'

'If you wouldn't mind. He's become a suspect in our investigation, but refuses to speak to us to clear his name. I understand this will be difficult for you–'

'It's not difficult at all. That man is a worthless piece of garbage. So ask any questions you like.'

Niamh Kennedy met Blake Horowitz soon after he arrived in the UK, having accepted a transfer from his then employer, an Australian property developer. She was pregnant with their first child by the time he left that company to take over as a project director at Triton Homes, and by the time he was assigned to the Hannibal Heights scheme they'd been married for six years and had two healthy sons, whose names I won't mention here. I managed to find a photo online of the boys posing with their dad, and they share his thick blond hair and confident grin.

'Why did you and Blake separate?'

'Because he cheated on me, over and over again, with lots of women. Girls, to be more specific. For years I blamed myself – I'd got fat since having the kids, I wasn't exciting enough for him in the bedroom, he was stressed at work, all that stuff. Those are the sorts of reasons he gave me, anyway, when I finally confronted him about it.'

'How did you know it was happening?'

'I think the pressure of coming up with excuses just got to him in the end. He tied himself in knots trying to explain why he couldn't stay at home half the time, why he couldn't miss certain work social events, why he was never there to help put the boys to bed. In the end I think he just stopped caring whether I found out. He got a lot sloppier with his excuses, didn't even bother explaining why he was arriving home at six in the morning. He actually seemed relieved when I challenged him about it.'

'Did you catch him in a lie?'

'Not exactly. It was more that I just realised one day how simple the explanation was, for all his behaviour. Like I'd been kidding myself for years, suppressing all my suspicion and fear and self-hatred. Then one night I was just lying there in bed, alone, as usual, and it dawned on me. Just staring up at the ceiling, it was suddenly so clear. I remember closing my eyes, smiling, laughing at how much of a fool I was. How I'd allowed myself to become 'one of those women', like a character in a soap. I started checking his phone after that.'

'And you found out he was having an affair?'

'Lots of them. A waitress from a restaurant we'd been to together, at least two graduates from his work, and a girl who as far as I could work out was a Bulgarian dance instructor he'd met online.'

'I'm so sorry.'

'Don't be. I divorced him, I got the house and half his money, and custody of the kids. I think I deserve that, in return for the decade he stole from me.'

She sounds defiant, but the note of fragility in her voice makes my heart ache.

'I hope you don't mind me asking you some more specific questions.'

'Shoot.'

'One of the graduates at Triton Homes was Katrin Gunnarsdottir, from Iceland. She's been missing for five years. Did Blake ever mention her?'

'It's not a name I remember.'

'On the night she disappeared she attended a party, and one witness believes Blake was there with her. I'm trying to work out whether that's true.'

'What date was the party?'

I told her, and she said she'd be right back. The receiver went quiet for a long time, and for a while I thought maybe we'd gotten cut off. Then, with a rustling of paper, Niamh returned.

'Tell me the date again?'

'The 31st of January, 2013.'

'Hmmm...' I pictured Niamh flicking through an old calendar, spread out on the table, full of pictures of cute cats or Star Wars characters.

'You still have records from back then?'

'I keep all my old annual planners. I put everything in them – shopping lists, to-do lists, appointments for me and for the kids, what Blake was doing that week at work. It's like a diary of all his lies.'

I will confess to feeling a little thrum of excitement. Perhaps Niamh's fastidious organisation was the slice of luck we needed.

'What does it say he was doing that night?'

'It was a Thursday night, right? We were away, travelling up north to visit my parents. We needed to be there on Friday because my dad was having a serious operation, and I wanted us to be there when he got out of hospital. I remember having to grovel to the school to let the boys take the day off.'

'Just you and the kids?'

'No. Blake came with us. I can't drive.'

The urge to simply reject what she was telling me was powerful. I realise now how wrongful convictions can happen, how detectives on the trail of a criminal can be compelled to disregard evidence or testimony that doesn't support their theory.

'Is there any way you could be wrong about that date?'

'I'm sorry, but no. We set off that evening, as soon as he finished work. There's no way Blake could have been at a party in London.'

This was the cast-iron alibi that Wim had told me about. And given everything Niamh had told me, how she felt about her ex-husband, there seemed absolutely no reason for her to lie to protect him.

'You said Blake had affairs with two graduates. Do you know their names?'

'I never found out. I didn't want to know. They just had code names in his phone. But you could figure out how he knew them from the content of the messages.'

'Can you remember the code names?'

'They were just initials. Perhaps I should thank him for not saving them as "Babycakes" or "Hot Legs".'

'What initials?'

I felt awful for pressing her, but I needed to know if there was any definitive link to Katrin.

'I'm sorry. I don't remember.'

'Do you remember anything else about the messages?'

'They were embarrassing. Like teenagers had written them. Sometimes pathetic flirting, sometimes really graphic sex stuff. I was shocked. He was saying things to these girls that he'd never said to me in our entire relationship. How he wanted to tie them up and whip them for being so naughty, that sort of thing.'

'I'm so sorry you had to go through that.'

'It's okay. Do you know the worst part?'

Niamh's experience of marriage sounded so terrible that I couldn't think of anything to say.

'It's the guilt. Of breaking up the family. The boys still hate me for it; like it's all my fault, not his at all. I was hoping that as they got older... ah well. You know that night, the night I finally realised what was going on? I'd had to explain to the boys why Blake wasn't there to read to them. I made up an excuse, as usual: "Your daddy is working really hard to earn us the money to live in our lovely house, and buy your lovely toys, and we all need to support him", blah, blah, blah. And then I said "but don't worry, I can still read with you", and' <sound effect signifying a redacted name> 'just said "nahh, that's okay". He wasn't nasty or spiteful about it. He just wasn't interested if it wasn't his beloved father.'

Niamh broke down in tears at this point, and asked to end the call.

Boys, if you ever listen to this when you're older, then I hope you can understand your mother's actions. I'm not asking you to hate your dad, but I am asking you to forgive your mum. Blake, if you're listening yourself, then I urge you again to contact us and give us your side of the story.

This episode will be broadcast on Katrin's birthday. She would have been thirty-one years old this year. I don't know if she spent any time with Blake Horowitz, or if he was with her the night she died. But I do know that everyone deserves a chance to grow old, and to learn from their mistakes.

27

EXTRACT FROM MARSH GROVE GAZETTE, 1996

CAR PARK ATTENDANT CONVICTED OF KILLING LOCAL TEEN

The trial of 32-year-old Eric Batson concluded yesterday with a guilty verdict, but the killer has avoided a life sentence for the murder of Samantha Napier, whose remains were recently recovered from Beechwood Canal after a three-day search.

There were gasps and shouts in the courtroom when the verdict of manslaughter was read out, after Batson's defence solicitor successfully argued that Mr Batson did not intentionally strangle his victim. Samantha's mother, Michelle Napier, who was attending the trial along with Samantha's fifteen-year-old sister, declined to comment.

Batson was arrested after new evidence emerged, ending a four-year hunt for the missing girl that has haunted the Marsh Grove community.

'This used to be a safe, quiet place,' said one local resident, also in attendance. 'Now I won't let my kids stay out after dark.'

It is understood that Batson was notorious in the area

around Ashgate Park, and would often go there after finishing his late shift at the shopping centre car park to offer to supply alcohol to teenage girls. The prosecution outlined how he persuaded Samantha to accompany him into the woods, but when she spurned his advances he strangled her before dumping her body in the canal.

Mr Batson has been sentenced to 12 years' imprisonment. A request for review is expected.

28

She didn't realise she was crying until a single tear splashed onto the paper. It landed right in the centre of the left-hand portrait, threatening to smear the ink. It didn't matter; Napier had an electronic version of course, the version she would soon share via the miracle of the internet with her listeners, with the world. She'd printed the hard copy to be able to look at it properly, to hold in her hand some physical trace of the girl she was hunting. To remind herself why she was doing this.

The printout displayed a pair of images, side by side. Katrin on the left, as she had looked shortly before her disappearance; on the right, an electronically aged version of the same photograph, simulating the effects that five years might have had on the missing woman. The changes were very slight, of course – wrinkles beginning to form at the corners of Katrin's mouth, a slight weariness around the eyes – but still, the simulation had had a powerful effect on Napier. Partly because, for the first time, she realised that Katrin might truly still be out there – but also that Katrin was dead, at least the Katrin that everyone remembered, the Katrin that brought joy to her friends and attracted an endless stream of admirers. In her place would be something broken, world-weary, traumatised.

Like Sam would be, if she was still alive.

But that was still better than the alternative. Napier would give anything for the photo on the right-hand side to be made real, for the person it depicted to stride into Hellendoorn's office one day and stun them all into silence with her very existence. She desperately wanted their quest not to conclude with a tragic discovery, a shallow grave.

A pile of bones dredged from a canal.

She felt the gnawing lure of alcohol in her throat and belly, and glanced forlornly at the fridge, which was bereft of such pleasures with only one week to go until the fight. Isaac had invited her over to his place in Maida Vale, but she'd decided against it, not wanting to tempt herself with the booze that would, inevitably, be in plentiful supply in his flat. She also wanted to focus on the case, on updating her notes, preparing for the next recording. Her apartment felt too small to contain the swirling thoughts in her head, and getting them all down on paper was the quiet catharsis she needed.

The trill of her phone cut through the silence like a hot scimitar, startling her. It was her landline, which rang so infrequently she'd almost forgotten she still had it. She scrambled to the hallway and lifted the receiver from its cradle, frowning. 'This is Elaine Napier.'

'Good. This is Blake Horowitz. Now you listen to me, you fucking bitch.' His Australian-accented voice was low and quiet, the rage and menace it contained reducing it to an almost reptilian hiss. She fought off the urge to hang up immediately, instead grabbing her mobile phone from her pocket as Horowitz continued. 'If you so much as breathe a word about me on your shitty little podcast again, I will come around there and shut you up personally.'

'Oh really? And what exactly does that mean?'

'It means I'll gut you like a fucking fish, you loudmouth whore.'

'I feel like we're getting off on the wrong foot, here.' Napier had dealt with hundreds of angry calls in her career, but she had to admit that she was shocked by the vitriol in his words. 'Is there anything specific I said in the last episode that you'd like to refute?'

'Spare me your sycophantic bullshit. Who even does that? Tries to turn a man's own children against him? Embarrasses two teenage boys at school, just for her own fame?'

'I didn't mention the boys directly.'

'Oh, fuck off. It isn't exactly hard to work out who they are when you're slandering me by name on your show. People listen to it, you know. I've had fucking hate mail because of you.'

'We're just presenting facts. It was Niamh's decision to allow us to interview her.'

'And you believed everything she said? You're even stupider than I thought. Let me guess: you're some lesbian man-hater?' His words were slurred, as though he was drunk.

'Mr Horowitz, I'd suggest you go to bed and sleep it off. If you want to call me tomorrow, we can start over.'

Horowitz's voice rose to a screech. 'I will most certainly not be fucking calling you tomorrow! There's nothing more to discuss. Just rest assured that if I hear my name mentioned again, I will sue you from here to Timbuktu.'

'Okay. Well in that case you won't mind if I play this on the next episode.'

She replayed the recording she had made on her mobile phone into the receiver, which opened with him threatening to gut her like a fucking fish.

There was silence at the end of the line. She could hear

heavy breathing, as though Horowitz had exhausted himself with his own anger.

'You'll be hearing from my solicitor,' he said eventually, and hung up.

Napier sagged against the door frame, feeling physically drained by the exchange. Her vision was misted by tears and she wiped them away angrily, pinching the bridge of her still-sore nose between thumb and forefinger.

She hadn't even thought about the impact on the boys. Not once.

Their mother's problem, right? And besides, this was journalism. Sometimes sacrifices had to be made to discover the truth.

Sacrifices like Katrin's reputation.

In her other hand, her mobile phone began to ring. She answered without looking at the number, assuming it was Isaac.

'Yep?'

'Elaine? It is Martina. I am sorry to call you so late.'

Napier blinked, surprised. Martina had been cold towards her since her outburst in training the previous week. She'd kept her head down in the subsequent sessions, barely spoken to anyone, concentrating on finishing the practice and making her exit as quickly as possible.

'Oh. Hi, Martina. That's okay, you don't need to apologise. Is everything okay?'

'Did you see the line-up was announced today?'

She'd completely forgotten. That afternoon, the match-ups for fight night had finally been announced. Surely to God they hadn't put her up against Sophie, after what had happened?

'Oh, no, sorry, I forgot to look. Who am I fighting? Is it Christina, or Lexie?'

'I am sorry. I tell him that this is unfair, but he says it is final. I cannot do anything about it.'

'I don't understand – who are you talking about?'

'Tony! I tell Tony to change the match-up, but he says it's – how do you say? – "set in stone".'

Napier closed her eyes. Now she understood. She could picture Weaver's grin, gleaming and sinister.

'Is it Nicola?'

A professional firefighter who regularly entered – and won – bodybuilding competitions. A woman who'd had shorts bearing the nickname 'Iron Maiden' specially embroidered for the competition.

'Yes! I say I am worried about you in this fight, but he will not listen. I am so sorry.'

'Don't be. I signed up for this. All I can do is give it my best shot, and see it through.'

She might have been talking about any aspect of her life. Her life as a whole.

'You are a brave one. I respect you, Elaine.'

'Thank you, coach.'

They said goodbye. Napier breathed a very long, deep sigh, and went back to the living room. She picked up the page once again, staring at the images, feeling as though she was gazing into the eyes of phantoms.

PODCAST EPISODE 12:

THE RABBIT HOLE

Lewis Carroll was the pen name of Charles Lutwidge Dodgson, born in 1832 in Cheshire in the UK. As well as a celebrated writer of children's fiction, he was also a gifted mathematician and photographer, and an Anglican deacon. He died in 1898 following a bout of pneumonia, two weeks before his sixty-sixth birthday.

I could continue pulling information out of Wikipedia, and tell you the entire life story of this very interesting character. But I will focus instead on the parts that might – or might not – be relevant to our investigation. Because there must be a reason our informant has chosen to use his name as their pseudonym. Our informant, who has so far shared with us two pieces of information.

One, their claim that they were at the party the night Katrin disappeared, and saw her getting into a white van with an eye on the side. This matches the description of the van driven by the Coughing Man, as related to us by Marcus Dobson.

Two, a piece of CCTV footage showing Katrin looking extremely agitated inside a lift, before fleeing from an unseen antagonist.

Lewis Carroll is, of course, famous for penning *Alice's Adventures in Wonderland*, as well as its sequel, *Alice Through the Looking Glass*. These stories were combined in the 1951 Disney classic, *Alice in Wonderland*, which helped to immortalise Carroll's dreamlike tales, and also their surreal, disturbing undertone. The movie, although ostensibly a kids' film, is creepy and unsettling; I still shudder when I think of the Walrus and the Carpenter, or of the Cheshire Cat's fiendish grin.

More sinister still are the rumours surrounding Carroll's fascination with children, fuelled by the many photographs he took of young girls. This subject matter comprises over half of his surviving work, and includes some nudes. Alice herself is said to be based upon a real girl, Alice Liddell, who was the daughter of Carroll's associate, and a model Carroll photographed on many occasions. Indeed, the Alice books have often been interpreted as Freudian tales of the loss of innocence, describing a descent into the subconscious mind and its forbidden, and at times maddening, desires.

But there are others who think this controversy has been completely manufactured. Nude portraits of children were popular in Victorian times, associated with purity and innocence rather than paedophilia, and the parents of the children Carroll photographed were always present at the event; remember, these were the days when cameras were clunky machines that required careful preparation and outdoor light for appropriate exposure, not sordid snaps hastily grabbed on a Polaroid in a dingy basement. Rather than some obtuse sexual confession, others have speculated that Carroll's magnum opus was in fact a satire on modern advancements in the mathematical field he loved.

Either way, perhaps *our* Lewis Carroll *is* trying to reference underage sex in some way – but how can this be relevant? Katrin was in her mid-twenties when she disappeared, a sexually active and consenting adult. So maybe Carroll is trying to tell us something about her childhood; but if that is their intention, why not just tell us openly, as brazenly as he or she has offered up their other tantalising clues?

Another significant fact about the real Lewis Carroll might be the stammer from which he suffered throughout his life. Katrin did not stutter. So is our informant trying to let us know that they themselves are somehow unable to communicate effectively? Some of our listeners have theorised that someone in the police force is responsible for the messages, and indeed it does seem unlikely that anyone outside of the investigation team could have gotten hold of the footage from the elevator; when I contacted the building manager myself, they were unwilling to cooperate. But again, this just seems too obtuse, one of the many straws I'm desperately clutching at. So many aspects of this case feel just beyond my reach, dangling threads that I can't quite grasp.

Lewis Carroll kept meticulous diaries, but for a four-year period they have been lost, with some alleging that this record was destroyed by his surviving family in their efforts to cover up a scandal involving the aforementioned Alice Liddell. The possibility of Katrin's diary being suddenly unearthed, a thick journal that unravels the mystery of her life and death, is surely remote. These days, young people keep their diaries in other ways: on Facebook, on Instagram, in the fragments of themselves they scatter across the internet like abandoned oyster shells.

Perhaps this is the biggest clue the person calling themselves Lewis Carroll is giving us: not intentionally, in the frustrating slivers of information they have dispensed; but accidentally, by pointing the searchlight of this investigation towards the dark matrix of the worldwide web.

Maybe, if we want to solve this, that's the next rabbit hole we need to jump into.

30

Napier had been to Venice, and thought it was overrated: a fish-scented tourist trap, the narrow streets crammed with people, the gondolas charging extortionate prices. Little Venice, on the other hand – the nickname given to the area of London near Maida Vale station, where the Grand Union Canal met the Regent's Canal close to where Isaac had recently moved – was quaint and pretty, and she was enjoying their evening stroll along the banks of the waterways as the sun began its descent.

Or at least, she was trying to. She couldn't relax, hadn't been able to for weeks. The sensation that she'd bitten off more than she could chew – the boxing match, the podcast, the burden of investigating a young woman's disappearance – was stronger than ever, like a gnawing itch on the inside of her skin.

'Earth calling Elaine…'

She realised she hadn't been listening to a word Isaac had said for at least the last minute.

'I'm sorry.' She offered him an apologetic smile.

'It's all right,' he replied through his thickening beard. 'I know you're distracted. It'll be better once tomorrow's finally out of the way.'

It was December 14, and that meant tomorrow was fight night. She was acutely aware of this, more aware than she'd been of anything for a long time, but still wished he hadn't mentioned it.

'I still think you should refuse to fight her.'

The idea had crossed Napier's mind more than once. In some ways, Tony Weaver's roguish booking had offered her a way out, an escape route that would preserve her self-esteem and integrity. She had been expecting to fight an opponent of similar size and skill, not a terrifying slab of chiselled muscle.

And yet.

'I think maybe Weaver thought I would. So even if I get battered – which I will – just going through with it feels like a victory.'

'You should call that moron and ask what he's playing at.'

She thought about the last time she'd seen Weaver, staring through the glass into a taxidermy shark tank as though face to face with his spirit animal. A violent man. A schemer. Someone who'd told her Blake Horowitz had been at his party on a night that it simply could not have been true.

Right now, there wasn't anyone alive she wanted to talk to less.

'You wanted to tell me about Katrin's Facebook account?' Napier said, changing the subject gracelessly.

Isaac frowned at her, a rebuke threatening to crystallise on his lips, before it dissipated into the chill air along with his misted breath. 'Well, as you know, it's still active,' he said eventually. 'Just like her Instagram account. Facebook own Instagram, which I'm sure you already know.'

Napier did.

'They have a process for when someone dies, but no one has actually followed the steps to shut down her accounts,' Isaac continued.

'Because she isn't necessarily dead,' said Napier. 'Her parents still post on her wall, every year, on her birthday.'

Isaac seemed uncertain how to respond. Around them, snow had begun to fall, each flake as fragile and fleeting as a person's life.

'Well, anyway, the point is that the accounts are active,' he continued eventually. 'Which means that her Facebook friends can see who her other friends are. So I reached out to Henry Wu, and he sent me a list. Guess who I found on it?'

'Lewis Carroll.'

'Got it in one. Which means that Carroll must have connected with her *before* she disappeared, because otherwise she couldn't have accepted the request.'

'Unless someone else is accessing her account. Someone who knows her password, maybe?'

'Like who?'

'Maybe Marcus knows it.'

'But why the hell would he do that? And why would he accept random friend requests from strangers?'

Every couple was different. What would seem a trifle in one relationship might be an unforgivable breach of trust in another. Perhaps it was routine for Katrin and Marcus to access each other's social media accounts. Napier remembered her ex-boyfriend, Warren, who had seemed genuinely shocked when she scolded him for opening her letters.

'Maybe he's investigating, like us. Part of his campaign to track down the Coughing Man. Is it possible to see when the friend request from Carroll was accepted?'

Isaac shook his head. 'When you connect with someone new it automatically notifies your other friends, but you can disable that, and she had.'

Napier chewed her lip, thinking. 'Who else is on the list? Henry, Abigail?'

'Yep. Also Jamal, Lukas, her parents' joint account.'

'What about Tony Weaver? Or Blake Horowitz?' She hadn't told Isaac about the call she'd had with the latter. She was annoyed at herself for feeling so shaken by it.

'Neither.'

'What about on Instagram?'

'Basically the same. Henry and Abigail are both on there, and Jamal, but Lukas and her parents don't have accounts. Neither do Weaver or Horowitz, as far as I can tell. She's following Weaver's promotion company, but it isn't following her back.'

Push Yourself Fight Club. Its logo, a silhouetted ring bell against a yellow flame, would be emblazoned across the ring tomorrow night. She wondered how much of her sweat and blood would be splattered across that insignia by the evening's end.

'If Lewis Carroll is connected to Katrin, does that give us a way to find out more about them?'

Isaac shook his head. The snow was thickening, teased by the rising wind into haphazard patterns that changed direction with each gust, like a huge flock of tiny white birds. 'It's a locked account. All you can see is the name, and that fucking picture of him in a suit and tie.'

'But if you were friends with them, you'd be able to see their friends too, and their posts. In other words, if we can access Katrin's account, we might be able to find out more about our informant.'

Isaac's face lit up, a pinkish beacon amongst the swirling snow. 'You're right. I hadn't thought of that.'

'But we'd need to get her password somehow. Which means I need to try to convince Marcus to talk to me.'

'Assuming he even has it.'

Napier exhaled deeply, feeling suddenly anxious. The cold

was beginning to snap at her ears and nose, nibbling at her fingertips like something hungry and desperate.

'Sunday. I'll call him Sunday, after the fight is over. I just can't face it today.'

Isaac nodded. 'Are you okay, Elaine?'

Another deep sigh escaped from her. *I don't know. What does that word even mean?* Instead she said, 'Don't worry. It's just the backlash getting to me a little bit.' Which was true: it wasn't just Dobson who thought they were sullying an innocent woman's reputation. They were receiving more and more emails and comments to that effect, almost a one-to-one ratio now with the messages of support and encouragement.

'Fuck 'em,' Isaac replied with surprising vehemence. 'You've already done more for Katrin than the police, or Hellendoorn have managed in five years.'

She nodded, feeling hollow, like a marionette whose head was being jerked back and forth. There was no feeling of success, or achievement. Recording the episodes was beginning to feel like a desecration.

'I'm going to head home, I think. Don't want to catch a cold the night before my sporting debut.' She forced a smile, which felt toxic on her face, like something vomited up and clinging to her lips.

Isaac stopped walking, and turned to frown at her again. His hand jerked outwards, seemingly involuntarily, like an urge to hold and comfort her. Then he withdrew it, and mumbled something about the weather being unpredictable, and asked whether she wanted him to walk her to the station.

'Don't worry. I think Warwick Avenue is just up there.'

They said an awkward goodbye, and he disappeared into the intensifying snow.

By the time she made it home, London was in the grip of a fully fledged blizzard, and the knot of anxiety in her chest felt swollen enough to burst. Her thoughts danced treacherously around the memories and fears that were feeding it: the pain of being struck in the face, the cold malice in Tony Weaver's grin, Sam's face, always there, always haunting her. Blake Horowitz's words, visceral enough to unnerve her: *I'll gut you like a fucking fish.*

The fight was tomorrow night, but she already felt beaten.

Her mind moved to Katrin, as always, wondering how she'd felt the night before her own bout. Napier realised that she hadn't asked any of the missing girl's friends how the loss had affected her. Perhaps she'd find out for herself, in less than twenty-four hours.

How did someone cope with being left broken and defeated?

She reached for her phone, and dialled John Hargreaves.

31

PODCAST EPISODE 13:

THE DRIVER

I'm recording this on a Friday night, the day before my white-collar boxing match. I'm nervous about it to say the least, restless and agitated; so instead of sleeping, like I ought to, I decided to call John H.

John was the driver of the Ryde that Katrin took home on the night of her disappearance, and it's taken us a long time to track him down. This is because John is homeless, spending some of his time in shelters and the rest on the streets of Stevenage. He has a mobile phone, and we got his number from one of the hostels he regularly stays in. Contrary to popular belief, a mobile phone isn't a needless extravagance for someone in John's situation – instead it's a vital means of contact with family, officials and outreach workers.

John was kind enough to allow me to record the conversation I had with him.

'Where are you staying tonight, John?'

'Depends how much money I make. Hopefully at the YMCA.'

'How long have you been homeless?'

'You sort of lose track of time. About two years, I think. Since I lost my last job.'

'When did you stop working for Ryde?'

'Oh, they sacked me straight away, as soon as the police started sniffing around.'

Ryde drivers can be terminated without notice, simply by being denied access to the app. John tells me that he briefly worked as a traditional cabbie, then a painter and decorator, then did household odd jobs for another app-based service provider, all to try to keep up rent payments on the small house he'd moved into when his marriage broke down, where Wim Hellendoorn first met him.

'Do you believe Katrin's disappearance had any impact on your relationship?'

'Oh, without a shadow of a doubt. People look you in the face and tell you they believe you, but you can see it in their eyes: a seed of doubt, like a weed starting to grow. I saw it in my wife's eyes, ever since the police first came calling. My wife, my kids, the detectives, everyone who knew.'

'That must have been very difficult.'

'It's still difficult now. None of my kids have spoken to me for years.'

When Wim interviewed John, his house had been covered with photographs of his children.

'But they must know by now that you're innocent?'

I told him that Wim and I ran the experiment at Katrin's old apartment, and that I agreed with the police that six minutes wasn't long enough for him to be responsible for her disappearance – not just because of the suitcase, but because of her attendance at the party afterwards, for which we've now found multiple witnesses.

'It won't make any difference. The truth is they just don't want to see me. I've become an embarrassment to them. This is my life now. I know I was never formally accused, but it still feels like I'm serving the sentence.'

I thought about his existence, about dark alleyways and the bitterly cold weather outside, and realised how insignificant my own concerns are, how frivolous I would sound if I told him I was keeping myself awake at night fretting about a charity boxing event.

'Can I ask you about that night? About your memories of Katrin?'

There was noise at the end of the line, voices raised in some sort of exchange, and the call cut out. I called him back.

'Is everything okay, John?'

'Oh, yeah, everything's fine. Just a bit of bother.'

John is now in his early fifties, and I suspect a lot more frail than the photograph I've seen of him in his Ryde-driving days. The slim, grey-haired and affable chap in the picture did not look well-equipped to deal with the sort of 'bother' that a life on the streets might involve.

'I was hoping to ask you about the ride you gave to Katrin. Whether you remember anything about it, about her.'

'Not really. She was just another passenger, and you go into a bit of an autopilot mode. I remember her being very pretty, and I remember offering to carry her case upstairs, but she was adamant she'd do it herself. It's difficult to be a gentleman these days – some women get offended if you offer them your seat on the bus. I mean, I don't want to upset you; I'm a feminist and everything.'

'That's okay, John.'

'... on her phone a lot.'

The call started cutting in and out at this point.

'I'm sorry? Could you repeat that, John?'

'I said she was on her phone a lot. Not that I minded – all the youngsters are the same. Some of the other drivers would mark them down for it in their customer review. But I always just gave everyone five stars.'

'Do you remember who she was talking to?'

'Well it's... you...'

'Sorry, John, you'll have to say that again.'

'... said it's funny you mention a party. I think she was arranging for someone to come and pick her up later that night. I remember thinking it was already late enough!'

'Do you remember who it was?'

'You'll have to forgive the sirens in the background. Never a dull moment here... what did... say?'

'I asked whether you remembered who she was on the phone to?'

'It sounds silly, but it might have been a Mr Wolf. Made me think of Little Red Riding Hood.'

Katrin's friends told us they suspected she was having an affair with an older colleague, who she called Mr Wolf. I can't prove it, but I think this person is Blake Horowitz.

'Are you still there?'

'Yes, sorry John. That's really helpful. There was just one other thing I wanted to ask you: do you remember being followed, at all? Perhaps by a white van?'

'Yes.'

The certainty in his reply startled me.

'Pardon?'

'Sorry... is that any better?'

'No, I heard you, I mean... you said you *were* followed?'

'Well, perhaps it was a coincidence. But a van was behind me for most of the journey, and then pulled up on the same street.'

'What kind of van was it?'

'I couldn't see it properly – its lights were on, and it was parked behind me. I remember being dazzled by the glare in my mirror.'

'But you think it was a white van?'

'Yes. A big old Ford Transit. It was still there when I pulled away to pick up my next customer.'

I could feel my pulse quickening. The pieces of this terrible jigsaw were, maybe, starting to finally slide into place. Katrin had arranged for Horowitz to pick her up, and take her to the party. If Lewis Carroll's statement could be believed, the Coughing Man could have followed them there, and picked her up after she'd fled from whoever she'd been arguing with in the CCTV footage – which might even have been Horowitz himself.

I asked John if there was any way we could meet in person, but the call cut out abruptly once again. When I called back, the line went straight to voicemail.

32

Napier awoke to find her sense of helplessness dispelled, like the previous night's snowfall by a tenacious morning sun. Instead, she was gripped by a feeling of cold clarity: the CCTV was the key. If she could get her hands on the rest of the footage, she would surely find out who Katrin had been arguing with. Something concrete in this story full of half-glimpsed mirages, of shifting sands.

She'd left a message for Yvonne Demetriou, but didn't hold out any serious hope that the DI would call her back. So instead she had decided to visit the building manager at Hannibal Heights in person. The building towered above her as she ascended the hill, seeming somehow to have grown taller since her last visit: a dark monument, with malign purpose glinting in its windows.

She was sick of feeling like this: paranoid, on edge. A little fish, sensing the approach of predators in the water. *Weaver. Horowitz. A man in a white van.*

And Nicola, of course.

Tonight was the night she had to battle the firefighter in front of a crowd of people. The thought drove a spike of fear into her stomach, a barbed lance that twisted with cruel relish each time her mind dared to drift away from it. But Napier scowled, and ignored it. It was time to face the music, no matter how frightening its tune.

To chew what she'd bitten off.

Was this how Katrin had felt, on the day?

That morning, she'd watched the footage of Katrin's fight once again. It was as though Katrin had been distilled into two videos: one showed a fearless woman, brave but beaten, someone that had ripped herself from her comfort zone, abandoned her native country to pursue a career miles from home. The other, meanwhile, captured the other Katrin: the one who seemed to be full of contradictions, unfaithful to her boyfriend, frightened and vulnerable. Hiding from her demons, trying briefly to confront them, failing, fleeing.

What demons would Napier be fighting later that night, embodied in Nicola Clarke? The ghost of her failures: her lost job, her non-existent love life, the children she didn't want. The mother she'd been such a disappointment to.

The missing girl she couldn't find.

The sister that was never coming back.

She wasn't going to be fighting Nicola, not really. Elaine Napier's enemy was, had always been, her expectations of herself.

When she reached the top of the hill, she realised how effortless the steep ascent had been; without noticing it, she had gotten into the best shape of her life. A tranquil confidence flowed through her as she walked past the fountain and its salivating menagerie.

Sometimes fights are won against the odds.

Sometimes missing girls come back okay.

The building manager's office was tucked away in a corner of the ground floor, close to the museum's entrance. Napier hadn't told him she was coming. Her knock was polite but insistent, as she planned to be.

'Come in,' called a weary voice from within.

She stepped into a windowless office so small and cramped that she couldn't believe someone spent their whole day inside. The desk occupied one corner of the space, and the chair facing it occupied another, supporting the bulk of an overweight and hassled-looking man who was younger than she had expected. He didn't turn to look at her. His gaze was fixed on the twin monitors in front of him; one was showing an episode of *Family Guy*, while the other displayed the feed from the various cameras around the property.

Like the one that had recorded Katrin, in the lift.

'Yep?' he said with an air of resignation, as though dreading whatever troublesome request she was about to burden him with. He didn't look away from the TV show, although he at least turned down the volume a little.

'Hi,' said Napier, mustering as much warmth as she could into her smile. 'Are you the building manager?'

'Yep,' he said again, continuing to stare into the screen, as though determined to devote the absolute minimum possible effort to this intrusion.

'In that case it's nice to meet you. I'm Elaine Napier. We spoke on the phone a couple of weeks ago.'

The man finally paused the show and swivelled his chair towards her, eyes lingering on the screen as he turned, as though she was tearing him away from very important work. He looked at her with the sort of expression she usually reserved for cold-calling salespeople.

Her smile remained resolutely intact. 'I wanted to look at some archive footage, from your CCTV cameras.'

The man gave a short grunt of what might have been recollection.

'But you told me the police had forbidden you to share it with me,' she continued, feeling as though she was spoon-feeding a particularly recalcitrant infant.

'Yep,' he said once more. 'I remember.'

'I came in person to convince you to change your mind. That footage could help to solve a crime.'

His face was a mask of scepticism.

'The footage shows a girl, who was attending a party at one of the apartments here. She disappeared that night. Her parents haven't heard from her for five years.'

'I already told you. The policeman who came said you'd be snooping around, and that I absolutely shouldn't help you.'

A police*man*.

So not Yvonne Demetriou.

'Did the officer give his name?'

Perhaps this detective was their mystery informant.

'Nope.'

'The thing is, someone already sent me the footage. It might even have been him. But it cuts off, at a crucial moment. Just before something I need to see.'

'Look, I can't send it to you. They might find out.'

Or maybe the building manager *himself* was Lewis Carroll. Although he didn't seem the literary type.

'What's your name?' she asked, cranking up her smile to maximum charm.

'Paul.' His use of syllables was so frugal it was beginning to be impressive.

'Well, Paul, what if you didn't have to send me anything at all? What if I just happened to see it, on your screen? Maybe I sneaked in and took a look while you were out, dealing with an emergency. That wouldn't be your fault, would it?'

'No. But you wouldn't be able to figure out my password. So it would be pointless.'

'Maybe I'm an expert computer hacker.'

'If you were, you'd have a better job.'

She took a step towards him, smile still fixed in place. He rolled his chair backwards, looking uncomfortable, but was quickly stopped by the wall behind him, which was empty except for a blank whiteboard and a *Hollyoaks* calendar hanging open on the wrong month. 'My point,' she intoned menacingly, 'is that I'm going to get that footage from you whether you like it or not. And if we do it my way, it will be much easier and faster. I suppose you wouldn't want to have to deal with an unexpected power cut, or a fire alarm, or a bomb threat. They all sound like an awful lot of hassle.'

'Look, I'm just doing my job.'

'And I'm doing mine,' she said, allowing the smile to suddenly dissolve.

All the colour had drained from Paul's face. When she reached into her satchel, he gave a little gargle of horror, as though he expected her to pull out a gun. Instead, she took out her wallet, from which she extracted the five twenty-pound notes she'd withdrawn earlier that morning. Eyes still locked on Paul's, she held them towards him. He took them from her in the manner you might snatch food from a crocodile's mouth.

'See?' she said, her beaming smile returning. 'Much easier. Now, if you could just fire up the footage you gave to the police?'

He whirled to face the computer. Despite the chill outside, she could see beads of sweat forming on his brow, and a tremor in his hand as he operated the mouse. Moments later she was looking once again at the very familiar clip.

'The policeman was here for hours, watching the videos,' Paul explained. 'Then he just gave me the timestamps for the part he wanted.'

'How long is it?'

'Just over four minutes.'

She nodded. The version she'd been sent was slightly shorter. She thought about asking him to skip ahead, but there was something almost ritualistic in watching it all the way through, feeling the anticipation squirming inside her like a nest of wriggling insects. Would the extra few seconds reveal what she wanted to see? What did she even expect?

A familiar face. A prime suspect.

Blake Horowitz.

Tony Weaver.

Lukas Serafinowicz.

The names had danced in her brain for so many weeks that they had become almost divorced from the men they belonged to. Seconds ticked onwards, and Katrin began to remonstrate with someone outside the lift.

Henry Wu.

Marcus Dobson.

Jamal Habib.

Napier bent forwards, her face inches from the screen. Paul backed away as though she was radioactive. In the video, Katrin shook her head, fear mounting in her face. Then she turned and ran. This was the point the original clip would have cut off.

Another person crossed the gap between the doors as they gave chase. The video quality was very poor, and they were visible only for the briefest of moments; but, even before her hand shot out to grab the mouse and rewind the clip, Napier knew who it was.

Katrin's assailant, who had chased the girl out of Hannibal Heights, never to be seen again.

Her new prime suspect.

Martina Mazziotto.

33

'Fucking voicemail again,' Napier cursed.

'Why don't you leave a message?' said Isaac, sitting next to her in the back of the Ryde. They were en route to the fight club venue in East London, the dark sprawl of the city rushing past their windows as though too busy to care.

'I've left three already.'

'Maybe she's busy getting ready for the show.'

'Or if the police have seen this footage, she might have been pulled in for questioning.'

'Would Demetriou even know who she was?'

'I just can't believe it.' Napier shook her head, screwing up her face in exasperation. 'It was definitely her, Isaac: she was there, arguing with Katrin that night.'

'That doesn't mean she killed her.'

'I know, but why wouldn't she mention it? Not once? "Oh yes, that missing girl you're searching for? I chased her out of a building on the night she disappeared, but I didn't think it was important."'

'Look, I know this is an unexpected development, and we need to think about what we do next; but right now you just need to concentrate on surviving your fight, okay? You won't be solving any crimes if you get beaten to a pulp.'

As he spoke, the taxi pulled up across the road from Netherworld, a former cinema converted into a venue for music gigs and sporting events.

'That's a lot of people,' she murmured.

Napier was supposed to have got there hours ago, leaving plenty of time to get ready and warmed up before the crowds started to arrive; but she knew she was fighting later in the evening, and hadn't really wanted to hang around backstage getting nervous or being psyched out by her opponent. So she'd anticipated that a small turnout of friends, family and insatiable boxing enthusiasts might have already gathered by the time she got there.

Instead, there were throngs of people queuing at the main entrance, easily over three hundred. The men wore smart suits, the women extravagant evening dresses, and they were all smiling as they chatted and smoked and vaped. It looked like something from a Guy Ritchie movie.

'Bloody hell, it's like a proper event,' Isaac said. 'Is there a back way you can sneak in?'

'Yeah, there is. I came last week for the weigh-in, and to sign my medical waiver.'

'You signed a *what*?'

She didn't answer as she clambered out of the car, almost forgetting her bag of gear. Most of it wouldn't be needed: the gloves and head guard would be provided, to make sure everyone stuck to the regulation equipment. She just needed to remember shoes, shorts, hand wraps and gum shield, as well as her sports bra and the T-shirt they'd printed for her with her nickname. Isaac had laughed when he'd arrived at her flat and seen 'Ice Queen' emblazoned across her back.

'Just a bit of free advertising for the show,' she'd said with a smile, turning to show him *The Frozen Files* logo on the front.

Such frivolity seemed light years away as they headed down an alleyway at the side of the building. She could hear music blaring through the grubby brick walls, and started to imagine walking out to the ring, truly picturing it for the first time. She'd step through the ropes, be patted down for foreign objects and laced into her gloves. Then there'd be no escape. She felt sick, swallowing hard as they approached the bouncer on the door.

'You a fighter?' the huge man asked. He was almost as wide as he was tall, like a block of fat and muscle crushed into a cube.

She nodded.

'What about you?' he asked Isaac, his face the personification of boredom.

'I'm her friend,' replied Isaac haughtily.

'You'll have to go round the front. Only fighters are allowed backstage.'

'Why?' Isaac protested.

The bouncer looked like he was holding back a deep sigh. 'Because that's the rules, mate. Like I've already told a dozen boyfriends, girlfriends, children, work colleagues, and a grandma who threatened to hit me in the balls with her walking stick.'

Isaac, once again woefully underdressed compared to the hordes around the corner, and now sporting a beard that could at best be described as 'unruly', looked at Napier in despair.

'I suppose I'll see you in the crowd,' she said in response.

He stuck out his bottom lip in exaggerated dejection. 'Well... good luck, I guess. It still isn't too late to back out. You could just come and get drunk with me instead?'

'Sorry. I'd love to. But I've got a date with the Iron Maiden.'

He smiled and squeezed her shoulder before he ambled away. She watched him go, then sucked in a deep, trembling breath.

'Nervous?' asked the bouncer, with the air of a man who'd had so many fights he could no longer remember the feeling.

'You would be too if you saw my bloody opponent,' she replied, and strode inside. Her nose was assailed immediately by a congealed, sugary odour that was half-cinema, half-nightclub, and she grimaced as her feet stuck to the ancient carpet. She headed in the opposite direction from the blaring music, not wanting to blunder out into the main arena and catch a terrifying glimpse of the crowd.

Neil, one of the male fighters, was heading the down the corridor towards her, already dressed in his ring attire. He smiled at her. 'You're late. Get ready and get out there quick – Spence is going to be on in a few minutes.'

'Where's the dressing room?'

'Up the stairs and to the right.' He pointed at a set of double doors, which she headed towards, ascending the curved staircase beyond to find herself in another backstage corridor. To her right, she could see several of the fighters congregated outside an open door. Two were chatting earnestly, while another sat slumped against the wall, eyes closed as she listened to music through enormous headphones.

Napier went through the door, anxiety like a billiard ball lodged in the back of her throat, robbing her of her breath. The dressing room was large, divided down the middle by a huge curtain. A young woman with a clipboard glanced up at her as she entered.

'Which side are you?' she asked through a mouthful of chewing gum.

'Er... I don't know?' Napier replied, then realised that everyone on this side of the curtain was wearing black T-shirts, unlike the white one she'd been given. The curtain was there to keep the fighters apart.

Serious business.

'White,' she said. 'My name's Elaine Napier.'

The girl nodded, crossing off her name from the list in her hand. 'You're late.'

'So everyone keeps telling me.' She could see Nicola in the corner, pretending not to have noticed her, looking lean and intense as she shadow-boxed. Napier tore her eyes away and headed to the other side of the room, changing as quickly as she could. By the time she was ready, the room was emptying, most fighters choosing to go and watch the first bout between hedge fund manager Ainsley and deputy head teacher Spencer. She followed them along the maze of corridors, feeling the ball in her throat growing larger.

She emerged onto the upper balcony, which had been reserved for the fighters and the backstage staff. The music blared, and the lights flashed and spun, a kaleidoscope of noise and sound ramming itself into her senses. She could smell booze, hear people below them shouting and cheering. The *Push Yourself* logo, garish and confident, hung directly opposite her on a large banner. She walked towards the railing, trying to keep her breathing under control as she looked down.

Below her was the ring. Spotlights danced across its black canvas, its sagging ropes making it seem well-used, like some old, blood-crusted gladiatorial arena. It was, somehow, simultaneously too big and too small: too dauntingly vast for her to contemplate standing alone at its centre, facing off against its only other occupant in a one-on-one duel while hundreds of people watched and cheered; yet far too tiny to possibly justify the fear, the trepidation, the reverence she felt for what was about to happen inside it.

Three two-minute rounds. Just six minutes.

That timespan seems to be haunting me, she thought as she stared downwards.

The ring was surrounded by tables occupied by groups of

suited men and glamorous women: the VIP seats, which Isaac had stubbornly refused to pay for. These provided the best views, of course, where you could quite literally taste the blood, sweat and tears of the competitors. As the lights dimmed and the music faded, her eyes were drawn towards one of these ringside vantage points. As a portly announcer clambered with surprising grace into the ring, smiling as he fiddled with his microphone, she focused on two people sitting side by side, their expressions unlike the smiles and laughter of the friends gathered around them. They were both staring into the ring with cold intensity in their faces, the expressions of people who knew what it meant to compete at an event like this.

'Ladies and gentlemen, welcome to White Collar Fight Club!' cried the announcer to a roar of applause, as Napier gazed down into the faces of Tony Weaver and Martina Mazziotto.

Of course they'd be here together. This was his promotion, and she was one of the coaches, not to mention his girlfriend. Napier didn't know why the sight of them was making her feel so uneasy.

Because Katrin disappeared from Weaver's flat. And because Martina might have been the last person to see her alive.

Maybe she was even her killer.

Napier felt a sudden surge of nausea spiking inside her, and dashed away from the railing, back down the stairs. She grabbed at the handrail as she stumbled towards the doors, battling back the urge to vomit, to purge her body of all the tension and doubt and terrible, stomach-squeezing anxiety. She barged past Neil on her way to the toilets, ignoring his 'Are you okay?', not stopping until she was safely in a cubicle with her head dipped towards the bowl.

What are you doing here, Elaine? What the hell are you trying to prove?

It came then, a great gout of bile, fleeing from her body like the last vestiges of her optimism. She stayed there until she was dry-retching, the violence of the spasms drawing tears from her eyes. Her ears were full of the muted sound of the crowd cheering, yelling, baying for blood.

Soon you'll have mine.

She staggered out of the stall and towards the sink, praying that no one would come in and find her like this. The splashes of cold water were welcome daggers in her face.

Is that how you felt, Katrin? Am I getting any closer to finding you?

That's when her phone rang. She'd kept it with her, in her pocket, intending to drop it off in the dressing room before her bout. She took it out to kill the call, then frowned when she saw the name on the screen.

Marcus Dobson.

She answered. 'This is Elaine Napier,' she said, trying to compose herself.

'Hi Elaine. It's Marcus.'

'Marcus, hi. It's good to hear from you. The last time we spoke you were angry with me.'

'I found him.'

'I'm sorry?'

'I tracked him down. All thanks to you. So I was just calling to apologise. For saying your podcast wasn't doing any good.'

A dreadful chill crept upwards from the soles of her feet, like wet fabric being dragged across her body.

'What do you mean, you tracked him down?'

'I found the Coughing Man.'

The chill seemed to wind itself around her neck, clammy and crushing.

'Marcus, what did you do?'

But the line went dead.

34

HOMEWORK ASSIGNMENT BY ELAINE NAPIER, 11B

The Funeral

Black dress mum says is too short
I listen to wretched music
And people crying
Surrounded by drunk relatives and flowers you wouldn't like
The priest has a lisp
I imagine you laughing
Mum frowns at me
(It's important to maintain our dignity)
Like you would have given a shit about these black-clad
strangers
And their sorrowful mumbling
Queuing in silence for the buffet
Some of them tell me they're sorry
I'm not sure what for
They didn't strangle you and throw you in a ditch
But someone did
My hatred burns for him
Every day

I imagine sticking hot pins in his eyes
Peeling off his skin
No one seems to care that he's still alive
Closed casket so all the sorry souls can pretend you're lying
there
As beautiful as you were
When you were the oldest
But I know there are just putrid bones inside
Bits of debris dredged up from the slime
People tell me you're at peace
But I know you're here, watching and
Screaming

35

PODCAST EPISODE 14:

THE END

Hello everyone. This is Isaac Jones, sound technician for *The Frozen Files* podcast. Elaine wasn't able to record this week, so I'm here to pass on her apologies... and to explain why this will be the last show of our series.

Elaine is currently recovering from a severe concussion, which she sustained during her charity boxing match this weekend. She fought very bravely in the first two rounds against a much tougher and more experienced opponent, before she was knocked unconscious in the third and final round. I travelled with her to the hospital, where she's still an inpatient at the time of recording. Although an MRI scan has ruled out any lasting damage, she's being kept in under observation for the time being. That's why Elaine isn't available to talk to you, but it isn't the reason we're ending our broadcasts.

We're cancelling the show because we received some very bad news this week. Specifically, we learned that a man has been attacked because of information we presented in an earlier episode. I can't give you any more specifics, other than to say that two lives have been irreparably damaged: one is the life of the victim, who has been left in a critical condition in hospital, and the other is the life of the perpetrator, who is facing a very lengthy prison sentence.

In Elaine's own words: 'I didn't start this show to ruin lives. I wanted to help people. So I'm ending it now, before any more damage can be done. I apologise, sincerely and profusely, to all of our fans, and to Katrin, to her parents and all the other people who loved her as much as I've grown to love her. I'm sorry I failed to find the truth.'

From my perspective, I just want to say, on air, that I disagree with Elaine. I don't think she has failed at all. I want her to know how proud I am of her, and what an incredible person I think she is. Elaine, we all just want you to rest and recover, and to come back stronger than ever.

By the time you listen to this, it will be Boxing Day, so I'm going to end by wishing you all a merry Christmas, and reminding you to cherish your loved ones.

A very merry Christmas to you too, Napes.

36

She shifted uncomfortably in the hard-backed chair. It was New Year's Eve, but there were no sounds of revelry, not there. Just the rhythmic, mechanical inhalations of the ventilator, punctuated occasionally by the machine's insistent beeping. Each electronic note was a reminder of how critically ill the man lying in the bed next to her was, of the technology that was now integral to his survival as it fed oxygen into his lungs and nutrients into his veins.

Of her culpability for his savage beating.

He would recover, they said. But it was a close-run thing. As well as the smashed ruin of his face, he had suffered multiple internal injuries, all of which would take a long time to heal. There was significant swelling to his brain, which was why he'd been placed into an induced coma. The doctors had pulled Michael Fairclough back from the brink of death's final, bottomless chasm – but he was still peering over its edge, flirting with that dark abyss.

She closed her eyes, but his face was still there, black and distended, a grotesque caricature of the person he'd been before. Then it faded, and another face appeared in her mind, one she'd seen only a day ago, smiling at her from the other side of a metal table in the prison visiting room. A serene smile, full of gratitude. That face was far worse. She opened her eyes again.

Marcus Dobson had listened to every episode of *The Frozen Files*. He'd heard Wim Hellendoorn talk about Focus Security Solutions, and how their logo matched Katrin's description of what she'd seen on a battered white van, loitering nearby as she waited outside the airport. Marcus had pondered the detective's words as Hellendoorn had told Napier, and their listeners, that Focus couldn't be responsible; that there were only two possible vans that could have been in use that night, and that both were in pristine condition, with drivers who didn't remotely match Katrin's description of the Coughing Man.

Marcus hadn't been able to shake the feeling that they were missing something. So he'd identified the former owner of the security firm, and paid him a visit. He'd masqueraded as a member of the podcasting team, and asked about the vans, whether there were any others out there that perhaps the company had sold. He'd found out that one such vehicle had indeed been sold for scrap, a couple of years before Katrin's disappearance. He'd learned the whereabouts of the scrap merchant, and found that the ageing owner was still there, running the place with the help of his sons. Marcus had asked, very insistently, about the van, and whether instead of scrapping it the old man had in fact sold it on, despite it being a rusted piece of junk that had no place being back on the road. The dealer had confessed that he'd sold it to a man named Michael Fairclough, who was the son of a friend of a friend, and needed a vehicle at an incredibly low price.

Fairclough was forty-two years old at the time of Katrin's disappearance, and had severe learning difficulties. He hadn't worked since leaving school, and still lived in the house he was born in, supporting his ailing mother. Having finally passed his driving test at the eighth attempt, he used her ancient Ford Fiesta to drive her to doctors' appointments and hospital check-ups, to run errands and do her grocery shopping. When the car had wheezed its last polluted breath, he'd decided to upgrade to a van, because his mum liked to visit the garden centre, and he often struggled to fit all their supplies into her little vehicle. Pot plants, ornaments, bags of gravel: Michael lugged them all through the tiny terraced house to the back garden, which he tended with as much care as he could, just like his dad used to. There was a rockery, a water feature, a collection of gnomes. He loved watching the starlings gather around the bird table every morning, although they would never stay there when he went out to play with them.

Napier didn't know why Fairclough had ended up on a plane back home from Iceland. Marcus, when she'd asked him, didn't know either. And he didn't care. What Marcus did know was that Fairclough was overweight, with scruffy hair and a thick beard, and that he struggled with his personal hygiene. He also knew that Fairclough had never bothered to paint over the Focus Security Solutions logo on the side of his grubby, rusted van. Marcus knew these things because he'd tracked Fairclough down, and been watching him for weeks, until he finally decided he'd got his man.

It hadn't been difficult for Marcus to break into Fairclough's house. Fairclough had remembered to lock the front door, like his mum had taught him to, but the back door to the garden was always left open until he went to bed, because the garden was his favourite place; even in winter he liked to wander out there to sit in the big chair and look at the gnomes, imagining that he was one of them, smiling and happy and surrounded by his friends.

Marcus had climbed over the back fence while Fairclough was in the kitchen. He'd brought a spanner with him, the largest one in his toolbox. He had started asking questions. When Fairclough hadn't been able to answer them, and started to cry and panic, Marcus had beaten him to a bloody pulp.

The doctors told her she was Fairclough's second visitor. The first had been Wim Hellendoorn, a couple of days previously. Fairclough's mother, too frail and infirm to leave the house, was now being looked after by a care worker.

She looked down at the forlorn, friendless figure in the bed, and felt guilt skewer her belly like a hot knife. His expression was strangely peaceful, but not the sort of peace anyone would wish for; this was the serenity of a mind vacated, consciousness driven from its husk by a hail of blows and kicks.

In the end she stayed for several hours, eventually nodding off in the chair and having to be politely awakened by a nurse. On her way home – to Meadowvale, for now at least – she stopped at the supermarket to pick up a few cans of beer and a big bag of Doritos. Back in the flat, she logged on briefly, feeling guilty that she wasn't checking *The Frozen Files* email account; she was leaving that to Isaac, who kept telling her how many goodwill messages she'd received, how hundreds of fans were urging her to get well soon and return to the show. Isaac, who was visiting his family in Leicester for New Year's Eve, and had invited her along. Isaac, who she'd lied to, saying she was visiting her cousin in Portsmouth for the festivities, and that she'd see him when she got back.

She looked around the clutter of her temporary home, feeling somehow ethereal, a person caught in transition between states. No job, no family, no podcast. No boxing match to train for.

A missing girl, still out there, somewhere.

She shook her head, determined to dispel all thoughts of Katrin. *And Sam. And Eric Batson.* Turning on the TV, she flipped quickly through the various annual reviews and live countdowns of the final hours before midnight, settling eventually on the delicious irony of a screening of *Rocky Balboa*. After an hour, the Doritos were gone, and she was drifting off to sleep on the couch.

There were a pair of knocks at the door. The first awoke her, the second affirming that the first hadn't simply been a part of her dream (a thick, treacly dream where she'd been searching, aimlessly, for something).

'Who is it?' she called, too tired and hollowed-out to even be frightened.

'FBI,' came a gruff reply, in a voice she instantly recognised. Smiling, she opened the door to find Wim Hellendoorn on the other side, wearing his usual grimy trench coat and fedora. He was holding a bulging Bargain Booze carrier bag in one hand, and a bunch of flowers in the other.

'I was just in the area,' he said.

'Are those for me?' she asked incredulously, suddenly conscious of the grubby dressing gown she was wearing, and the high likelihood that there were bits of Dorito in her hair.

'Not all of them,' he replied, the plastic bag clinking as he shook it. 'But I suppose I can spare a bottle.'

'I meant the flowers.'

'Oh.' He thrust the bouquet towards her. 'Yep. Thought you might need cheering up.'

'Thank you. I do.'

'Me too.' He didn't wait to be invited inside, squeezing past her and throwing his jacket onto the heap that had accumulated on the chair in the hallway.

'Nice place,' he said, and seemed to mean it. 'You been here long?'

'Only a few months. It was only meant to be temporary, while we recorded the show.' She gestured towards an empty chair next to the dining table. 'Make yourself comfortable. I'm afraid I haven't really got any food to offer you.'

'Don't worry, I've already eaten. My signature dish: pasta à la microwave.'

'You and I have a disturbingly large amount in common, Wim.'

She managed to find a vase for the flowers, two clean glasses, and a corkscrew.

'What shall we cheers to?' she asked as she poured the wine, a bottle of pinot that she suspected came from the most bargain end of the retailer's selection.

'To your health,' he replied, clinking his glass against hers. 'How are you feeling, after the fight?'

'I'm fine. Although I don't really remember much about it. Everything after the entrance is a blur.'

'I'm not surprised. That woman was huge. You fought really well.'

'So you've seen the video?'

He grinned. 'I was there. A window opened in my schedule, so I thought I'd come and cheer you on in person. Interesting choice of entrance music.'

'I didn't know you were a Spice Girls fan.'

'I'm not.'

'Anyway, I'm surprised they let you in. There was a strict dress code, you know.'

'You'd be surprised at how well I scrub up.'

Their banter continued like that for a while. She felt a warmth surrounding them, something healing and mutual; she enjoyed his company, and knew that he enjoyed hers. But the unspoken undercurrent was always there, like something lurking at the bottom of a deep pool. It was Napier herself who gave voice to it, after they opened a second bottle, as the clock ticked past 11pm.

'So... do you think it's him?'

'You mean Fairclough?' He held her gaze.

'The nurse told me you'd visited him in hospital.'

Hellendoorn leaned backwards in the chair, wincing as he looked upwards at the ceiling, as though even thinking about Fairclough was causing him physical pain.

'I visited his mother, too,' he said eventually. 'Do you know why he went to Iceland?'

Napier shook her head.

'He wanted to see the gnomes. They're called the *huldufólk*. He read about them online. She said he became quite obsessed about it, and although she knew she'd struggle without him for a few days, she thought it was better to let him get it out of his system. She thought he'd earned a break from looking after her.'

He shifted his gaze back towards Napier, a remorseful look in his eyes.

'No, I don't think it's him,' he said. 'I spent so long searching for him; but now I realise I wasn't searching for him at all. I was searching for an idea, a bogeyman. A monster from a fairy tale. Like his gnomes.' He sagged forwards, his expression wry and strained. 'And I failed. Not just where Marcus succeeded, in tracking Fairclough down. I failed when I made the Coughing Man the pantomime villain, all those years ago.'

'The police are digging up the garden at his mother's house.'

'I know,' Wim replied sadly. 'She was really upset when I went to see her. She kept asking how she was going to get it fixed before he came home.'

'I should go and help her rebuild it,' Napier muttered. 'Not that I expect her to forgive me.'

Hellendoorn's face became stern. 'This is what I don't understand, Elaine. How you can blame yourself for what's happened.'

'Because it's my fault,' she said pointedly. 'I wanted to reopen this case, to draw new attention to it. To see if I could make a breakthrough. And instead, all I've done is wreck two more lives.'

'Then *own* it.' She was surprised by the harshness in Hellendoorn's stare. 'If you truly believe you created this mess, the only way to make up for it is to *keep going*. You knew that reopening this case might mean upsetting people, finding out uncomfortable truths.'

'But we haven't found *any* truths. At least, nothing concrete. Just broken pieces, blurred reflections. The whole thing is like...'

Like being lost in the mist.

'That's our job, Elaine. We're investigators.'

She closed her eyes, shaking her head. Immediately, Michael Fairclough's face returned to her, his eyes hidden behind bruised flesh and cracked sockets, yet still seeming to scald her with their accusations.

'I can't, Wim. I'm sorry.'

He nodded, saying nothing. Then he reached into his pocket and took out his mobile phone, placing it on the table between them.

'Can I play you something?' he asked.

She frowned, then nodded. He fiddled with the archaic device, and a recorded message began to play. It took her a few seconds to realise that the voice belonged to Gunnar Olafsson, Katrin's father.

'Hello Elaine. Wim called me. It was good to talk to him – we haven't spoken for many years. I told him I was once very angry he could not find Katrin. But the truth is, he did much more than I ever could. All I do is sit here and drink, surrounded by my regrets, haunted by my daughter's ghost. But do I lift a finger? Where does all this aimless rage get me? Katrin is gone, and the only people trying to do anything about it are Wim, and you. So I wanted to ask you to please not give up, like I did. To keep searching. Without you, Katrin is nothing more than the memory of a bitter, angry old man.'

The message ended. 'He still hasn't paid me,' muttered Hellendoorn as he slid the phone back into his pocket.

Napier said nothing as the detective poured her another drink. The clock on the wall edged closer to midnight, towards another new beginning.

She took a deep breath.

'Did I ever tell you about my sister?' she said.

37

VOICE RECORDING BY ELAINE NAPIER

I'm recording this on my way to visit you. I don't know why. Don't worry, I'm not going to put it on the bloody podcast or anything. I suppose it just feels more like someone's listening, even if it's just the dictaphone.

I was worried people would think I was bonkers, muttering into my hand while I walk around a cemetery, but it turns out the place is completely empty. Maybe it's the freezing weather; not quite chilly enough for snow, but cold enough to leave a dusting of rime over the headstones, making everything sparkle like I'm in one of the old fantasy films you used to love; *Legend*, was it, where Tom Cruise and everyone else look like they've had a bucket of glitter chucked over them? We must have watched that about two hundred times.

Or maybe everyone is still just recovering from their New Year's Eve hangover; either way, I'm the only person here. Unless the ghosts are all hiding behind their graves, sniggering at me. I suppose I shouldn't joke about that stuff in a place like this, but it's what you would have done, isn't it? Tried to find the humour in every situation, even if it pissed mum off no end.

Not that she stayed annoyed with you for very long. Because

you were the favourite; don't worry, I'm not blaming you for it. Or maybe I am, even if that's unfair – maybe that's why I haven't been to see you for years. Maybe I need to accept that I'm just a petty, jealous bitch, and that I *did* give a shit what mum thought, and that I used to think that what happened was your own fault, just a little bit, for always flirting with everyone, for being too trusting.

The truth is I was angry with you for years, after you died. Not just because you were prettier, cleverer, funnier. Because you got to meet our dad, even if you were too young to remember him.

Because you left me on my own.

Anyway, that's all in the past, now. I'm sick of this bitter, twisted version of myself. Maybe I have Katrin to thank for that; God, that poor girl's parents don't even have a gravestone to visit. I can see yours now, right next to mum's, the path overgrown and crunchy with frost as I'm walking up. I remember her arguing with me about the lettering on it – she thought gold would last longer, but I thought it looked tacky, and you wouldn't have liked it. What an opinionated little shit I was. And it turns out she was right – the gold looks nice. It really is a beautiful place you've got, here in your quiet corner under the trees, with the branches all sagging downwards towards you as though they're kneeling to pay their respects.

I'm sorry I don't come here more often, Sam. It's just hard, you know? I can't visit you without standing right next to mum's grave, and I can't bring myself to forgive her, I just can't. She treated me like garbage until the day she died. Maybe that was her way of dealing with what happened. And oh look, here's dad's tombstone on the other side, a man I never even met, a nice little happy family all lined up together. And then here's Elaine, the outsider, the troublemaker. It feels like we were all destined to die, and I've just cocked up my part somehow. Always the black sheep.

Maybe that's what the podcast was all about, I don't know. Maybe I was trying to solve Katrin's case because I never got over what happened to you. They sent me to see a shrink for a while after you disappeared, you know. I said some horrible shit to him; you would have loved it. I just felt like I was a car he was trying to repair, or something. They all just desperately wanted me to be *fixed*, as soon as possible. None of it worked, all his mumbo jumbo, all the teachers insisting I could always talk to them if I needed to. The only thing that worked was finding out what happened to you. 'Closure', as they say on the telly. Once Batson was arrested I had a target for all my anger.

I'm sorry for mentioning his name. But that pervert got what he deserved, and I'm not sorry, not one little bit. It felt like the only thing I could do for you.

So, anyway, that's why I've decided to carry on with the show. I don't believe in heaven, or God, or souls, or redemption. But Gunnar and Anna are still here, and they deserve to know what happened to their daughter. Even if all I can do is give them someone to hate.

Like I said, I don't actually think you're up there, watching over me. I don't think you can hear any of this, or that you're anything other than long dead and gone, a teenager who never got a chance to grow old and cynical.

But thanks for listening, Sam.

38

PODCAST EPISODE 15:

THE FIGHTER

Hello everybody. I want to thank you all, for the unbelievable amount of support you showed me while I was hospitalised. I've heard people in this sort of situation use the word 'overwhelmed', and it always seemed like a bit of a trite thing to say, but I really mean it; when Isaac told me to check the forum I couldn't believe how many kind messages I had received. I feel as though I don't deserve them, not one bit: my injury was nothing serious, and I sustained it participating in a silly amateur boxing match, which no one forced me to do. But, even more so, I feel I don't deserve your support because I *quit*. I decided there would be no more episodes of *The Frozen Files*, and didn't even have the courage to tell you myself.

And still, you were there for me. I am humbled, and I am more grateful than you will ever know.

And now, after a lot of soul-searching: I'm back.

Before my impromptu Christmas break, Isaac told you that we'd had some bad news. I need to own it, and to tell you what's happened. Marcus Dobson, Katrin's boyfriend, has hospitalised a man named Michael Fairclough, who he believes is the Coughing Man. Michael, a forty-seven-year-old man with learning difficulties, acquired a van from a scrapyard in 2011. The vehicle used to belong to Focus Security Solutions, and still had their logo – the symbol of a watchful eye – painted on its side when he used it to drive home following his flight back from a trip to Iceland, the same night Katrin disappeared.

This was enough evidence for Marcus, but it isn't enough evidence for me. Police have dug up the garden at Michael's home, and have found nothing to link him to her disappearance. But the fact remains that Michael is now in a coma because of this show, because of information that I gave out. That's why I wanted to abandon the podcast: because I never wanted to cause any harm to an innocent person.

But now I realise that it's unavoidable. When you reopen a case like this, when you pick at scabs and probe at five-year-old wounds, you are *bound* to cause pain. You are destined to become unpopular. I've already been threatened with termination, with physical violence, because of things I've said on this show. So, to Michael Fairclough, who travelled all the way to Iceland because he decided he wanted to see the *huldufólk*; to the mother who he looked after before the attack; even to Marcus Dobson, who I know is consumed by grief for his missing girlfriend, I say this: I am truly, truly sorry for the harm you have suffered.

But, together, we're going to finish this thing. Because we owe it to Katrin. No matter what happens, I am making a promise that no stone will be left unturned until we find out what happened to her. If that means I have to become the most hated woman in podcasting, then so be it.

So my investigation restarted today, in the Tate Modern, where I met with Martina Mazziotto. Martina coached me for the boxing match; although it ended in defeat for me, without her expertise I wouldn't have survived for more than a few seconds. Martina, who is a semi-professional MMA fighter, also coached Katrin before her own bout, and indeed was the person who recommended that I talk to Jamal Habib, way back before episode three was recorded. She has always been good to me, and is a great coach and an even better fighter, and I have a lot of respect for her.

But in the weeks leading up to Christmas, I learned some other things about Martina.

One is that she's dating Tony Weaver, who runs the promotion that she fights for, as well as the white-collar fight club that both I and Katrin competed in. You'll remember him from episodes four and eight.

The other is that, when I was able to obtain the unedited version of the CCTV footage from the Hannibal Heights elevator – where Katrin is depicted hiding, and then running from an unknown assailant – I found that the person chasing her along the corridor was none other than Martina herself.

I wanted to give Martina an opportunity to explain her side of the story, before I and everyone else jumped to conclusions. So we met, and we walked amongst the works of Rothko and Dalí and Monet and Pollock. We explored a temporary exhibition by Olafur Eliasson, which included a corridor filled with artificial vapour that made it seem as though you were walking through thick fog. If this seems an apt metaphor, there was an even better one to come: the artist had placed a water fountain in a pitch black room, illuminated only by occasional split-second strobes of lighting, leaving the weird shapes formed by the cascading water imprinted briefly on our eyes. Fleeting fragments, bursts of data that our brains struggled to make sense of, quickly superseded by another flash.

We went for coffee, where I told Martina that I intended to record and broadcast our interview. I'm sick of asking for permission. She looked uncomfortable, but said yes.

'I'll get straight to it, Martina. I know you threatened Katrin on the night of her disappearance. Why didn't you tell me?'

'I didn't know, Elaine! That this was the night she went missing. I just thought she never came back to the gym because we argued.'

Her eyes were wide and beseeching.

'And the police haven't questioned you about it?'

She shook her head. I know the police have the video footage, because the building manager told me he'd shared it with them, so I genuinely don't understand why they don't seem to be interested. But I've grown tired of trying to contact them for comment; as far as I'm concerned they can continue their investigation, and I'll continue mine.

'Can you tell me what happened?'

'She was with Tony. I walked in on them, in his bedroom.'

Tony has never mentioned this to me. He implied that he could barely remember whether Katrin even attended the party at his apartment.

'Were you and Tony an item, back then?'

'Yes. We broke up for a while, because of this. Only two years ago did we get back together.'

'What time did this happen?'

'I arrived very late. I wasn't going to come, but then I changed my mind. Hardly anyone was there. Just some people asleep on the couch and on the floor. Passed out with drink and weed.'

'And you found Tony and Katrin in bed together? Were they having sex?'

'No. Just lying on the bed. But close. Talking, maybe kissing, I don't remember.'

'And you were angry?'

'Yes.'

'What did you do?'

'I shouted at Tony. I... maybe also threw some things at him.'

'Did Katrin try to stop you?'

'No. She just left.'

'But you saw her again later, in the corridor?'

'It was maybe only two minutes after. I walked out and she was just there at the lift.'

'What happened?'

Martina, who is short and lithe but with broad, imposing shoulders, looked down into her drink like a scolded child.

'I shouted at her. I called her names.'

'Like what?'

'Slut, whore, bitch. I am ashamed, that I said these things. But I was angry.'

'Then what happened?'

'She became angry with me too. She said it was Tony's fault, that I shouldn't be shouting at her. I said it takes two for this to happen. She said nothing even happened. I did not believe her.'

'So you chased her.'

I couldn't tell if Martina's gaze was weighted with guilt, or because she was hiding something.

'What is the phrase... I saw red.'

'Did you hurt her?'

'No! She ran to the stairs, and I left her. I went back to the apartment and threw everybody out. I was so tired I just slept there, on the couch.'

'Did Tony explain himself?'

'I threw him out too. I said I didn't care if it was his apartment. He could go and find somewhere else to stay for the night.'

'Do you know where he went?'

'No.'

'And you've never asked him, Martina?'

'You are saying... that maybe he did something to her, that night?'

'I'm just saying that Tony never mentioned any of this. It seems like a bit of a big coincidence, doesn't it?'

The muddle of Martina's emotions was starkly visible in her face, as though her features were suddenly at war with each other. Her eyes glistened as she told me, through gritted teeth, that she had to leave. People turned to stare when the café's door slammed shut behind her.

Afterwards, I went back into the museum for a little while, for one last look at some of my favourite pieces. I stopped in front of Picasso's *The Weeping Woman*, but I didn't think about Martina's tears, or about whether or not I could trust her. Instead I just saw Katrin, because I see her everywhere, all the time.

39

It was bitterly cold as they ascended towards The Animal House. Isaac rubbed his hands, bemoaning his lack of gloves, but an uneasy silence soon fell upon them again. Perhaps it was the sombre purpose of their visit; they were about to go to a man's apartment to accuse him of committing murder. Or maybe it was the unspoken yet obvious absurdity of Isaac's attendance; if Tony Weaver reacted badly to Napier's insinuations, what did she realistically expect her friend to do about it? They were about to confront a man who had pummelled countless opponents into submission with his bare hands, who wore his own extracted teeth on a chain around his neck.

The fountain wasn't running when they reached the main courtyard, the animals staring forlornly down at the crust of ice that had formed on the murky water. They hurried past it, and Napier buzzed Weaver's apartment.

'Don't come up with me,' she said to Isaac while they waited for a response. 'That'll look too antagonistic. Wait in the museum, and I'll call you if I need help.'

'But what if he surprises you?'

'He's not going to physically attack me, is he? The man is a wealthy boxing promoter for God's sake.'

'Then why am I here?'

There was a burst of static, then Weaver's voice crackled down the line.

'Is that you, Napier?'

'Yes.'

'I'll buzz you in.'

'I'm here too,' interjected Isaac, leaning into the microphone. 'I'm her friend, Isaac. I work on the show with her.'

'Ahh. You're the prick that's been impersonating my voice.'

Isaac didn't respond, unsure how to react.

'Whatever,' Weaver continued. 'The more the merrier.'

Napier glared at Isaac, who shrugged innocently as the door began to buzz at them. They pushed through it into the now-familiar main hallway of Hannibal Heights. Napier summoned the lift, and together they headed up to Weaver's apartment.

She had proposed meeting in the museum once again, but Weaver had refused. 'If you want my side of the story, you can come to me,' he'd said when she'd called to forewarn him about the previous episode. If he'd been angry, he hadn't allowed it to show in his voice. His tone had been as calm as an ice-cold lake as he'd specified that the rendezvous was to be their last, and not to be recorded or even transcribed. His apartment was on the fifteenth floor, and Napier realised as they exited the lift that it was likely they were walking along the same corridor down which Martina had pursued Katrin nearly six years ago. She felt the familiar sense of following in ghostly footsteps, Katrin's presence strong and insistent, willing her to assemble these final clues.

They were close, now. She could feel it.

Weaver was standing in his doorway when they arrived. He didn't say anything in greeting, didn't even flash them his intimidating smile. He just turned, and led them into a large, open-plan apartment with a sprawling L-shaped couch, a granite-topped kitchen island, an expensive-looking glass coffee table. The room was dominated by an enormous TV set, and a set of sliding doors that led out onto a large balcony with a breathtaking view across London. Weaver stepped through them and stood, gazing out across a tableau of countless cranes and skyscrapers, of dozens of housing developments just like this one, in various stages of construction.

Of a city, never finished.

They followed him outside. 'Thanks for talking to us, Tony,' Napier said awkwardly.

'I haven't said anything yet,' he replied, not looking at her. Despite the cold, he was wearing a sleeveless vest top, and she could see the tattoos that covered his arms, snakes and barbed wire and tendrils of curling smoke all intertwined. His muscles were like chunks of stone, packed tightly beneath his ghost-white skin.

'If you're angry, I understand,' she replied evenly. 'Our last episode cast a lot of suspicion on you. But I have to report the facts. And you didn't tell me you were with Katrin that night. So I hope you can understand why I might be struggling to trust you.'

He turned towards her. His expression remained impenetrably flat, but something was smouldering in the dark pits of his eyes. 'People need to move on from their mistakes, not be constantly reminded of them. The dead should stay buried.'

Napier held his gaze, trying to think of a response.

'Katrin was never buried,' cut in Isaac. 'And she might not even be dead. Unless you know differently, that is.'

Napier, caught between them on the balcony, could feel the barely masked aggression in Weaver's eyes as they flicked towards Isaac, like two cruise missiles locking onto a target.

JON RICHTER

'This your muscle, is it?' Weaver asked in a low voice, not looking at her. His stance shifted subtly, one foot planting behind the other, his shoulders loosening like hydraulic machinery. She had a sudden, horrifying vision of Isaac hurled to his death, splattering on the pavement below like a piece of carelessly dropped fruit.

'Look, Tony, we didn't come here to upset you. We just want to hear your version of events. It might be completely untrue that you and Katrin–'

'No, it's true,' Weaver said without hesitation. 'I was with her that night. We talked. She was interested in me. In my life, my career. My winning smile.'

Napier saw the necklace dangling around his throat, as always. 'Is it true that Martina kicked you out of your own flat after Katrin left?' She winced at her choice of words, not wanting to enrage him further. But if she expected indignation or denial, she didn't get it.

'Yes. I wouldn't mess with Martina. Would you?'

All the time, Weaver's eyes remained fixed on Isaac. She hoped, prayed, that her friend didn't say anything stupid.

'Where did you go?' she asked carefully.

'As I recall, I ended up spending the night at the allotment. I slept on the floor of the shed.'

'And you never saw Katrin again?'

Weaver shook his head slowly. 'As you keep reminding everyone: she disappeared.'

She opened her mouth to reply, then cringed as Isaac interjected once again. 'Look, Tony. I'm sorry if I upset you. Please just try to see it from our perspective. We're trying to find out what happened to Katrin, and it turns out not only was she *here*, in your apartment, on the night of her disappearance, but–'

Weaver moved with lightning speed, the precision of a swooping hawk. One moment he was standing in front of

Napier, a coiled spring of hostility. The next, he had darted past both of them, whirling to grab Isaac around the throat from behind in a vicious choke hold. Napier stared, horrified, as Weaver leaned to whisper into his ear.

'Just stop. Stop speaking. Do not speak again. Is that clear?'

Isaac managed a weak nod, his face rapidly turning the colour of spilt blood. Weaver's forearm was locked around his neck, the other arm clamped behind it, making Isaac's head look as though it was trapped in some sort of industrial press.

'Please, Tony,' Napier implored. 'Don't do this. He doesn't mean any harm.'

Weaver's gaze swivelled towards her, his grip not loosening. 'But nevertheless. Harm is being caused. Don't forget that I *listen* to your show, Elaine. And in your last episode you said you didn't care anymore if you upset or hurt anyone. Like an omelette with eggs, eh? Well, that works both ways.'

Something toxic glinted in his eyes, a mixture of rage and sadistic pleasure, as he tightened the hold. Isaac gave a strangled cry, frozen like a small animal caught in the claws of a merciless predator.

'Tony, just let him go, for God's sake!'

Now the smile, that gleaming metal grin. 'On your knees, bitch,' Weaver hissed.

She caught Isaac's eyes. 'I'm sorry,' he mouthed. She shook her head. *Don't be.* Then she sank to the floor, the wooden deck of the balcony slick and cold as she knelt on it.

I'll make you sorry, you fucker.

'Please. Just let him go. I'm begging you.'

Weaver's smile faded suddenly, as though having got what he wanted he realised he didn't want it after all. He dropped Isaac as though he was diseased, a look of disgust on his face. Isaac slid to the floor, wheezing and coughing. Napier helped him to his feet, her arm around his shoulders as they limped back inside the apartment. He sank onto the couch, desperately trying to recover his breath.

'No parting shots for me?' Weaver was still on the balcony, addressing his words out across London's grey, bustling panorama. 'Or are you happy, now you've made me look like the monster? Well you can put this in your next fucking podcast: *I didn't do it.*'

Napier turned to him, staring at the wide, rippling outline of his muscled back.

'You know what, Tony?' she snapped. 'You don't get forgiven for doing terrible things just because you're philosophical about them. When I first met you, I thought you were fascinating: a tortured soul, a warrior with a brain. But you're not. You're just another slab of meat, with bad teeth.'

She turned to help Isaac to his feet. Weaver stood silently as they left his apartment, staring out at the skyline, where black clouds were coagulating like a blood clot.

40

MEMO TO PRISON GOVERNOR ROBERT IRONS FROM SENIOR PRISON OFFICER ARUN PATEL, 2008

Re: Death of prisoner
HIGHLY CONFIDENTIAL

In response to your request for more information on yesterday's incident involving prisoner Eric Batson.

As you know, the prisoner was taken to hospital following an attack that took place in the changing rooms, where he sustained nineteen stab wounds. Prison Officer Carmichael was the first to attend the scene, where he found the offender lying in a pool of his own blood, and raised the alarm. Lockdown procedures were initiated immediately as per standard operating protocol. The murder weapon, a sharpened plastic comb with the teeth removed, was discovered nearby, and has since been handed over to the police investigation team. Upon questioning, none of the other prisoners admits to having witnessed the incident or having any idea which person or people might have committed the crime.

However, Batson's cellmate Darren Beale has made contact with me separately, claiming that Officer Carmichael is known to be (Beale's words) 'completely corrupt'. He also claimed that

Officer Carmichael committed the murder himself, using a makeshift weapon to divert suspicion towards the inmates. Clearly these are grave allegations, and although Beale is unable to provide any tangible proof, we need to take them extremely seriously. For what it's worth, Beale seemed extremely agitated when we spoke, and it isn't beyond the realms of possibility that this was an arranged 'hit' on Batson; however, we also cannot discount the possibility that Beale himself is the culprit, and this is a clumsy attempt at misdirection.

We will continue to support the police in their investigation, as well as progressing our own discreet internal enquiries. The changing rooms remain off limits, preventing access to the showers and causing a small amount of unrest amongst the population of B-Wing. This situation will be monitored, with the facilities expected to be available within the next 24 hours. Staffing levels will be temporarily increased following the necessary budgetary approval, although Officer Carmichael has been given two weeks' paid leave, ostensibly to allow him to recover from the trauma of discovering the victim but in reality to ensure he is available to fully participate in the investigation.

I will ensure you are kept directly informed of any further developments.

Very best regards,

Arun Patel

Senior Prison Officer

41

PODCAST EPISODE 16:

THE LOOKING GLASS

Since our last episode, we spoke with the boxing promoter Tony Weaver, who was not willing to allow us to record or transcribe the interview. Suffice to say that Tony is no longer a friend of the show. However, he remains adamant about his innocence; although he now admits that he spent time with Katrin on the night of her disappearance, he claims that after Martina threw him out of the apartment he went to sleep in the shed at his allotment, where I first met him.

While we ponder our next move, we've also spent more time trying to track down some of our story's absent players. L, the besotted work colleague who apparently invited Katrin to the party that night, remains uncontactable, still away on his backpacking trip. I told you recently that the gloves were off in terms of protecting people's identities, so we're going to disclose L's full name, to see if that can rouse a response from him; Lukas Serafinowicz, please get in touch with the show, as we are desperate to hear your information.

Another character whose silence is conspicuous is Lewis Carroll. We haven't heard anything from our mysterious informant since they sent me the abridged CCTV footage, and although that clue certainly opened new avenues of enquiry for us, many questions still remain: why send me footage with the most crucial segment edited out? Why send me footage at all? How did Carroll obtain it in the first place?

Thanks to Wim Hellendoorn's brainwave, we've had a small breakthrough on that front too. This is a recording of my recent conversation with Katrin's mother.

'Hi, Anna. It's Elaine Napier. I'm sorry to disturb you.'

'That's okay. We're glad you're back!'

'That's kind of you. I'm sorry I was gone for a little while.'

'I'm sure the boxing didn't help. I always told Katrin she could get hurt doing that nonsense.'

'It was just a bit of concussion. I'm fine now.'

We made small talk for a little while. She told me that Gunnar is fine, and that her online store is doing very well, before I explained the reason for my call.

'I want to ask you about Katrin's Facebook account. We think someone might still be accessing it, and I wondered if you had any idea who that might be?'

'Oh. Well, er, yes. It's me.'

This took me by surprise. 'Okay... can I ask why?'

'I know it sounds terrible, like I'm some sort of ghastly prying mother. I just wanted to find out everything about her, anything that might help to explain where she'd gone. So I managed to guess her password. And then I just carried on logging on, to see if there were any messages or friend requests or whatever... I know it sounds silly, but it just felt like there was this tiny part of her that was still alive, out there on the internet.'

'It doesn't sound silly at all, Anna. Do you sometimes accept the friend requests?'

'Yes. I don't really know why. I suppose I should get them to close the account down.'

'Do you remember accepting a request from someone called Lewis Carroll?'

'That's the person who's been messaging you? This mystery man?'

'Or woman. We're assuming the profile picture isn't genuine, so it could be either. But yes, the account is friends with Katrin on Facebook. So we're trying to work out who Lewis Carroll is.'

'Do you think they could be the person who...' She didn't finish the question. I tried to imagine the trauma she must go through every time she has to find words for what happened. *The person who took my daughter. The person who killed my daughter.*

'We're not sure. But it would be really helpful if you could allow us to access Katrin's account. That would enable us to see Lewis Carroll's friends list, so we might have a better chance of tracking them down.'

I don't doubt that Lewis Carroll is listening to this episode. They'll probably delete their account as soon as they realise we're tracking them like this. That's why we've already done all the work before broadcasting it. Because, Lewis, Katrin's mother *did* give us the password. And we used it to find out some interesting facts about you.

The first is that you befriended Katrin only three months ago, soon after this podcast began airing. Katrin's mother must have accepted the request.

The second is that you only have three other friends. These are Tony Weaver, Blake Horowitz and – bizarrely – John Hargreaves, the Ryde driver.

Both Weaver and Horowitz have refused to talk to us about this. I'm still trying to work out the full implications, but in this increasingly tangled web, this feels like an important thread. Meanwhile, we've left messages on John Hargreaves' phone, but he hasn't yet called us back. John, if you know anything at all that might help us, then we would urge you to please get in touch.

Lewis Carroll, you can, of course, end all this confusion and speculation by simply contacting us yourself. But, as usual, I suspect you won't; instead I think you'll just continue to listen, and plan your next move.

42

Her head nodded towards the paper as though she had become entangled in the diagram she had scribbled there. It was a 'mind map', and its scrawled arrows felt like barbed hooks tugging her downwards by the eyelids. She was tired, and frustrated, the jumbled chart perfectly reflecting her scattered thoughts. It wasn't yet late enough to go to sleep, but perhaps just a quick nap, to reset her mind.

Some time later her phone rang, and she jerked awake. 'This is Elaine Napier,' she slurred groggily as she fumbled the handset towards her ear.

'It's me,' said Isaac. 'We need to go to see Wim Hellendoorn. He wants to meet us in his office, straight away.'

She didn't remember getting ready, but found herself in her car, with Isaac in the passenger seat. He was unable to provide any further details about their mysterious summons; Hellendoorn's message had been cryptic, and troubling. At some point, they arrived. The trees surrounding the detective's office seemed like eager spectators, the rustling of their naked branches like excited whispers in the dark. Napier and Isaac headed towards the side entrance that led directly into

Hellendoorn's office, rather than the peeling red front door that stood as little more than a sad, rarely-used monument. The wind picked up as they approached, howling at them with malicious glee.

When they were a few paces away, they realised that the door was ajar.

'Oh shit,' muttered Isaac. 'Maybe we should call the–'

But she had already barged through into the office, gripped by disturbing visions, caring only about Hellendoorn and what was going on inside his lonely, crumbling house. The room was dark, and as silent as a sepulchre; the only sound was Isaac's breathing behind her as her hand pawed at the wall, searching for a light switch. Ahead, she could barely discern the silhouetted shapes of drawers and filing cabinets.

And someone sitting at the desk.

'Wim?' she called, just as Isaac found the switch. The wind picked up again, shrieking its amusement as the room was soaked in an eerie yellow glare. The person at the desk was indeed Hellendoorn. He was staring straight at them, his jaw hanging open as though surprised to see them. He did not move.

'Wim, what the hell–' she began, stupidly, to say, even as she saw the blood that oozed down the sides of his face, staining his shirt bright red as though he was dressed for a Christmas party. 'Oh God,' she mumbled, rushing towards him, her mind rejecting what she saw even as she perceived it, trying and failing to divert the terrible image from her consciousness straight into some hidden, repressed area of her brain. To protect itself from the horror.

'Oh God,' Isaac echoed beside her, as they stared together at the wreckage of Hellendoorn's skull. The top of the detective's head had exploded outwards from within; pinkish chunks of bone and brain matter were splattered across the desk, his chair, the carpet, and the shoulders of his trench coat, as though someone had dumped a gristly stew all over him. They gazed in disbelief at their friend's lifeless body, as behind them the door started to bang, the wind blowing it open and closed, open and closed, as if in mockery.

There were too many inputs, too much for her to absorb: the laughter of the wind, the door's rhythmic crashing, the sightless orbs of Hellendoorn's eyes, like paperweights taken from his desk and stuffed into the ruin of his face. The blood-caked crater where his razor-sharp mind had once been cocooned. That gaping chasm seemed to draw her in, her eyes snared by the force of its violent annihilation.

Look what you've done.

She turned to Isaac. 'What do we do?'

But he wasn't there. Instead, only a smile hung in his place, detached and impossible, widening diabolically as it floated amongst the shadows. There was a glint of metal as it shaped words in the darkness. 'Don't ask me. I'm just a slab of meat.'

Grinning like a Cheshire Cat.

The wind roared in delight, and the door crashed, and she awoke from the dream, sweat smearing the pencil lines on the paper beneath her head. Her mind was a maelstrom of relief, horror, confusion.

As she reached for her phone, noticing it was nearly 11pm and that she had several missed calls, she realised then that the door was still banging. She scrambled to her feet, her heart pounding as loudly as the unrelenting hammering sound, wondering if perhaps a vestige of the nightmare still clung to her brain, like the image of Hellendoorn's corpse, vivid and terrible.

But no. This was no dream. She was awake, in her living room, and someone was knocking insistently on her front door. She gulped down a deep breath, and called out, trying to keep the fear from her voice.

'Who is it?'

'It's Martina! I have been calling you!'

She breathed a deep sigh of relief. But still the nightmare refused to entirely dissipate, and she was cautious as she opened the door, keeping the latch in place.

'What do you want?' she spoke into the crack, beyond which she could see her former coach standing anxiously on the threshold, dressed in a dark hoodie. The tufts of pink hair emerging from beneath made her look like something from the pages of a manga comic.

'I am sorry to disturb you, Elaine… I just really, really wanted to talk to you. Can I come in?'

Napier inhaled slowly, trying to calm her mangled nerves. What was she afraid of? She'd had a stupid dream, that was all. Because she'd been shaken up by their visit to Tony. Because this case was forcing her to meet with violent people, people who scared her.

People like Martina.

She glanced again at her phone, and saw that the missed calls were all from Martina herself. With another steadying breath, she opened the door. 'Come in,' she said. Martina entered, looking uncomfortable, and hovered in the living room until Napier told her to sit down.

'Can I get you a drink of anything?' Napier asked, trying to sound friendly. 'You'll have to forgive me if I look like garbage – I just dozed off, and had a nightmare.'

'I've been having nightmares too,' Martina said earnestly. 'I keep thinking about what you told me.'

'About Tony?'

'Yes. I have not listened to your show before, Elaine. It is hard for me, because my English is not perfect. I do not always understand when people speak quickly, or use certain words.

But I listen to your last episodes, including the one which I am in. And I've been thinking hard about it.'

A troubling thought crept into Napier's mind. 'Can I... ask how you found out my address?'

'I got it from the gym membership records. I hope you don't mind; I just had to talk to you.'

It would be so easy, she thought, *so easy for someone to track me down, to show up here in the dead of night. To stick a gun in my mouth and blow my head apart, just like Hellendoorn's, in the dream.*

'Martina, why did you come here?'

The Italian shifted anxiously on the couch. Napier realised then that the expression she'd seen in Martina's face wasn't awkwardness or embarrassment; it was fear.

'I think Tony has maybe done some bad things,' she said eventually. 'He doesn't talk about them with me, not any details. But I know he has had disputes with people, in the past. People that are not around anymore.'

'What sort of people?'

'Business associates.'

'You mean boxing business?'

Martina shook her head, but did not answer.

'But you weren't afraid of him that night, when you kicked him out of his own apartment.'

'I didn't know him so well, back then. But now I see him making phone calls, meeting with strange men. He has drugs at the apartment sometimes, even once a gun.'

'Why are you telling me this?'

'I can't stop thinking about that night. I didn't know, I swear it, I didn't know that the night I chased her was the night she disappeared.'

'Okay, so Tony is into some dodgy activity. It doesn't give me much to go on. If you think he took Katrin, what happened to her?'

Martina glanced around as though paranoid that Weaver was, somehow, watching them. 'Do you know about his... what is the word... his garden?'

'You mean the allotment?'

Martina nodded. 'He spends a lot of time there. Sometimes he goes to check on it, out of the blue, in the middle of the night.'

Napier felt her body grow suddenly cold, as though a ghostly presence had crept up from behind and wrapped her in its embrace. 'Are you saying what I think you're saying?'

Martina just stared at her, her eyes wide.

43

'Elaine? This had better be good,' Hellendoorn croaked, his voice exactly like someone who had been roused from a drunken sleep.

'Wim – I'm glad you're okay,' she blurted out before she could help herself.

'I'm not that old,' he mumbled. 'There's still a bit left in the tank.'

She laughed, then remembered the nightmare, and the sound died in her throat. 'I dreamed you died. We were getting closer to the truth, so he had you killed.'

'Who?'

'Weaver. I think he did it, Wim.'

'Okay. Well I assume you have more than a dream to go on, if you're calling me at...' There was a pause while he checked his phone, or perhaps his alarm clock. It was just after 1am. 'Jesus,' he said.

'I think he killed her and buried her in the allotment.'

'Why?'

'Martina came to see me tonight. She was talking about

some of his business activities, his associates. She said some of them go missing.'

'And you think they're all there, pushing up cabbages?'

'I think we should check it out.'

'The police will check it out, if you have any hard evidence. But I'm guessing you don't.'

'I don't.' And, if she was honest with herself, there was another reason she didn't want to contact Demetriou with this. She wanted to be there when something was found; to see the truth come out of the ground, in person.

'So I'm guessing you're calling me because you want to go and dig around there yourself.'

'You're good at this.'

Hellendoorn sighed deeply at the other end of the line. 'When?' he asked, apprehension in his voice.

'Tomorrow night, with Isaac. Gives us a chance to buy some equipment.'

'I'm not sure they sell camouflage paint and night-vision goggles around here.'

'I was meaning three spades.'

'You know you won't be able to talk about this on the show, Elaine. This is a felony.'

'I'll worry about that when we've found something.'

'I'm still not clear why you're suddenly so convinced Weaver is involved.'

'Do you know what he said to me, when we visited him last week?'

'What?'

She paused, feeling another chill pass through her. 'He said the dead should stay buried.'

44

PODCAST EPISODE 17:

THE RIDDLE

I was wrong. Lewis Carroll didn't delete their Facebook account. Instead, they contacted us again. Just like before, the email came from murky_water@xmail.com, with a subject line all in lower case: 'why is a raven like a writing desk?'

This is another reference to *Alice's Adventures in Wonderland*, a question posed by the Mad Hatter at his infamous tea party. The message contained an answer to the famously unsolvable riddle, a questionable pun that the real Lewis Carroll would probably have been proud of:

'they both carrion decomposition'.

But I was more interested in the series of five hyperlinks immediately beneath, the first four of which took me to news articles about unsolved crimes. The first detailed a botched armed robbery in 2007, where one of the two masked criminals was shot dead by a petrol station owner who had an illegal firearm hidden under the cash desk. The other thief beat the man to death with a cricket bat before escaping with less than £300 in cash, and was still at large at the time of the report.

The second was about a drug dealer whose torso was washed up on the bank of the Thames in 2008. Although the arms, legs and head were never found, he was identified by the distinctive 'ACAB' tattoo on his back (a common prison tattoo that stands for 'All Cops Are Bastards') which someone had modified with a blade to instead read 'SCAB'.

The third was an appeal for information about a boxing promoter who disappeared in 2010. Sean Roach was a small-time player who had been accused of fixing fights, and had fallen foul of some local gangsters. Although all of the cases so far had been horrifying, this was the first one that sent a chill down my spine – because as I scrolled down the list of Roach's business dealings, I could see that he was a former business partner of Tony Weaver.

The fourth link mentioned Tony again, this time as one of several local businesspeople horrified by the disappearance of one of the tenants at their business centre in 2014. Emre Erdogan ran a stationery wholesalers, and his rented unit was directly adjacent to the gym Tony was running at the time. Emre was described as popular and friendly, and the article was accompanied by a photo of a long-haired young man with a wide, beaming grin. Once again, the police investigation seems to have reached a standstill.

The final link took me to a YouTube video in which Tony is interviewed about the rise in popularity of white-collar boxing. He is charismatic, charming even, flashing that formidable smile at every opportunity while he extols the benefits of boxing training for fitness and confidence. Underneath the five-minute clip, which has only a handful of views, someone has added a comment that says, in lower case letters: 'killer interview' followed by a thumbs-up emoji.

The commenter's name is... you guessed it. Lewis Carroll.

The clear implication here is that Tony was somehow involved in these four unsolved cases. But, as usual, Carroll's accusations are vague and unsupported; there is no hard evidence, and we must remember that our informant's scattergun aim has previously been turned on the Coughing Man, and even on Martina Mazziotto.

Just like the email's subject line, this is a riddle that doesn't make any sense.

But I can't help recalling something Tony said to me weeks ago, when I met him in the museum – a turn of phrase that Lewis Carroll seems to be referencing in their email address.

I have a murky past.

I'm starting to wonder if it's about to catch up with him.

45

The last time Napier had visited Meadowvale Community Gardens, it had felt like a sanctuary, an unexpected oasis nestled amongst the city's bustling tangle of roads and train lines and office blocks. She'd enjoyed its tranquillity, and resented the sound of distant trains rumbling past like the ominous spectre of civilisation. But that had been during the day; now, just after midnight, the place's serenity took on a new form, warped by the darkness into something desolate and unwelcoming.

The surrounding fence was rusted and imposing, dotted with sodium lights that did little to penetrate the gloom beyond. The silhouetted shapes of trees were like grasping claws, and Napier imagined dozens of owls watching from amongst their gnarled branches, glowering their disapproval at this skulking band of intruders who approached like ghouls might descend upon a graveyard to plunder its fresh cadavers.

But there was not a single hoot from these imagined avian onlookers; indeed, the quiet was so thick it was stifling, and the jangling of Hellendoorn's skeleton key in the main gate's padlock startled her, making her think of rattling chains and shambling apparitions. Even the distant tracks had fallen silent, as though the frost that covered the ground had somehow spread to the trains themselves, sealing them in place.

'Fuck me, it's cold,' muttered Isaac, his voice and the squealing protestations of the gate as it creaked open slicing through her reverie. 'I wish you'd picked a better time of year for this. The ground will be rock hard.'

'No time like the present,' she quipped, trying to mask her irrational fear. Or perhaps not so irrational; who knew what truths they were about to dig up, amongst the frozen bulbs of Tony's garlic and onions? She didn't want to think about Katrin's bones, but the image of a grinning skull leered at her nonetheless, as though her mind's eye was taunting her. Feeling uneasy, she directed them to Weaver's tiny patch of land, and the three of them sank their spades into the dirt.

'I saw a documentary once, about Richard III... remember, the one they dug up from a car park in Leicester?' No one reacted, so Isaac continued. 'They hit the jackpot in literally the first spot they tried. Maybe that will happen to us.'

'Just keep your voice down,' hissed Hellendoorn. 'We don't want to get arrested.'

Isaac fell into a sullen silence, and soon their digging was the only sound: the metallic scrape as shovels plunged into soil as hard as Isaac had feared; the soft crumbling as it was heaped nearby; occasional grunts of effort from Hellendoorn, who despite his age worked the fastest of all of them. Napier's thoughts jerked briefly towards images of forced labour, of malnourished prisoners compelled into mindless excavation in some arid compound, but despite the monotonous rhythm of their activity her mind did not drift very far from the cold reality of their situation. Her breath misted in the air as their spades skewered the earth, and with every clump of soil her heart and stomach tightened horribly, expecting to see a protruding rib, a jutting femur, a fragment of pelvis gleaming in the moonlight.

But they found nothing. Minutes passed, and the minutes became nearly an hour, then over an hour, and suddenly it was almost 2am. Around them, Tony Weaver's allotment had become a deep cavity, like an open grave.

It was Isaac who spoke up first. 'Look, Napes... I don't think there's anything here.'

'We can't give up yet,' she replied, taking the opportunity to lean tiredly on the handle of her upright spade. 'What's if there's something just a few more inches down?'

'We need to be sure,' agreed Hellendoorn. 'But I could do with a smoke break.'

'Go on, I'll join you,' said Isaac enthusiastically, following Hellendoorn as he clambered out of their crudely dug pit.

'I didn't know you were smoking again,' Napier chastised.

'Working with you, is it any wonder?' Isaac retorted, but not unkindly. There was a flash as Hellendoorn's lighter sparked into life, his and Isaac's faces hellishly up lit by the red glow. Napier watched the tips of their cigarettes, dancing separately in the darkness, occasionally coming together like a pair of watching eyes. She tried not to think about the task that awaited them in refilling the hole once they were done. And what exactly was 'done'? Isaac was right: they couldn't keep digging in vain all night. Dejectedly, she thrust the shovel once again into the ground, which was at least more forgiving now they had removed its frozen upper layer.

There was a wet tearing sound, and the spade sank into something soft and yielding.

She froze. It was strange, to feel such excitement and such dread at the same time. The others hadn't noticed yet, and she almost felt compelled to keep quiet, as though if she said anything to them then whatever she had found would wink out of existence like a magical artefact.

And besides, she thought as she sank to her knees in the dirt, scrabbling around the blade of the shovel, *it's probably just a bit of nothing*. Some buried rubbish, perhaps, or a mouldy old bit of carpet.

But it wasn't. It was a shoe box. It was soggy and aged, and the spade had easily punctured the lid. Its contents rattled softly as she picked it up, as though it was full of plastic toys.

'What's that, Elaine?' called Hellendoorn as he and Isaac hurried over, cigarettes tossed aside. 'What have you found?'

Slowly, almost reverently, she opened the container. There was no rising howl of wind, no portentous flash of lightning. Just that same thick silence, as though the air had congealed around them, as they peered into the box.

'Is that... what I think it is?' Isaac murmured, half to himself.

For a moment, Napier couldn't figure out what he meant, because the box's contents seemed utterly baffling to her. Dozens of tiny colourless fragments, like shattered crockery, or unpopped kernels of white corn. The situation suddenly seemed surreal, and she felt a powerful sense that she'd slipped into another dream, as though she might collapse into the quarried earth heaped around them and wake up still asleep at her dining table.

She blinked, trying to clear her head, and suddenly was very certain of what she was looking at.

'Bloody hell,' Hellendoorn said, the implications seeming to enter his brain at the exact same moment as they entered hers, brutal and disturbing.

'Why would...' Isaac began, allowing the thought to trail off.

In silence, they stared together into a shoe box filled with dozens of extracted teeth.

46

TELEPHONE CALL, 2008

'Is this Elaine Napier?'

'Yes. Who is this?'

'I got your number from Frank.'

'Oh.'

'He said you wanted to buy something.'

'I... yes. He said you would give me a price. Did he tell you–'

'He did. It'll cost you fifteen grand. Still want it?'

'I can't think of a better way to spend my inheritance.'

'Frank says you're a reporter.'

'Don't worry, you can trust me.'

'So Frank says.'

'Did he say anything else about me?'

'That he owes you a favour.'

'Well, he does. Does that get me a discount?'

'You're already getting one. I don't like nonces.'

'So... what happens next?'

'I'll be in the Lion in Stepney Green tomorrow at 2pm. Be on time or I'll be gone.'

'Do I need to bring the money with me?'

'Half. I thought you people knew how this worked.'

'Not my area of expertise.'

'Clue yourself up. There are bad people about.'

47

PODCAST EPISODE 18:

THE MONSTER

It's been just over a week since I dug up Tony Weaver's allotment in the middle of the night.

If this comes as a bit of a surprise, it's because I didn't tell you about my plan; I couldn't, because I was trespassing illegally, not to mention vandalising public property. If I'd found nothing, I probably would have replaced the soil as best I could, and never mentioned anything about it.

But I did find something. The shoe box I unearthed contained sixty-eight human teeth, mainly molars. So far, since I turned it over to the police, I've had very limited information from them, so I don't yet know who they belonged to. It's possible that at least some of them belonged to Tony Weaver himself. But an adult has only thirty-two teeth, so that explanation covers less than half of the bizarre treasure trove.

What I do know is that Weaver himself is in custody, assisting the police with their investigations into various unsolved crimes. I know that this includes a full excavation of the allotment, which is now cordoned off with police tape and being treated as a crime scene.

I also know that police are investigating the necklace that

Weaver wears around his neck, because I made sure they knew about it. Whether these teeth are genuinely his own, as he told me, or whether they belong with the rest of his grisly collection, remains to be seen.

Sadly, I also know that none of the teeth have yet been identified as belonging to Katrin.

So where does this leave us? We have a prime suspect under arrest, a man who has seemingly murdered at least a handful of former business rivals, criminals and other unfortunates, taking their teeth for reasons I suspect even he cannot explain.

We have a lead police investigator who has finally agreed to meet with me next week, which means I may be able to provide some more concrete information in our next episode.

And we have a halfway-plausible narrative for what happened on the night of Katrin's disappearance. Here's what I think might have taken place:

John Hargreaves dropped her off at home, where she left her suitcase before immediately heading back out again. She possibly got a lift from Blake Horowitz, although his ex-wife claims he has a cast-iron alibi for that night; either way, she attended a party at Tony's flat, in the very same building she had helped to design. She and Tony had a romantic interlude, or perhaps were just talking intimately with each other, before Tony's girlfriend appeared and angrily chased Katrin out of the building. Tony himself left shortly after, and that's when he encountered Katrin again, perhaps wandering outside, trying to get a cab home. Maybe he persuaded her to join him in a taxi... or even just dragged her into nearby woodland.

What happened next, I don't know. We can only hope that the truth is revealed during his interrogation by police.

Meanwhile, we still have other loose ends to tie up. Can Lukas Serafinowicz corroborate this story, if and when we ever track him down? Who is Lewis Carroll, and why did they lead me on such a merry dance before finally pointing me – vaguely, obliquely – towards the truth?

As regards the unlawful excavation of the allotment site, I want to apologise to Meadowvale Community Gardens for any distress caused. I may yet face criminal prosecution as a result of my actions. But I'd be a hypocrite if I said I wish I'd left the authorities to handle matters. Because the truth is they wouldn't have done anything; I had no evidence, no proof at all to present to them. Just a hunch.

Sometimes that's a good enough start.

48

It was the last day of January, and London had been squeezed in winter's merciless grip for weeks. The air was dry and bitter, the ragged clouds occasionally coughing up swirls of powdery snow that drifted and settled and then faded away, like gatherings of tiny ghosts. Napier always thought of the homeless at this time of year; not because she was blessed with a saintly conscience, but because it was impossible to ignore them in a city like this, the tragic multitude crouched in doorways or shivering on street corners, wrapped in whatever assortment of clothes and blankets they'd been able to accumulate, their eyes cursed with a kind of pleading horror as they asked, please, for any spare change.

'You should give them food. She'll only spend the money on booze,' Isaac had chastised when Napier dropped a few coins into a battered coffee cup held beseechingly upwards by an elderly woman, her head bowed to the ground beneath it next to a cardboard sign that read '*no home, war refugee*'.

'I don't blame her. I fucking would too,' Napier had retorted.

That had been a few days previously, and she hadn't thought about the old woman again until, out of the blue, John

Hargreaves had called her. He was still sleeping rough, he said, but back in London now, and wondered if she'd be able to meet him at the home of a friend to discuss something. He apologised for not returning her call sooner, and said that he had some more information regarding the case. She didn't press him about the Facebook account, or tell him about the developments with Tony Weaver they had broadcast the previous day – she could go over those with him in person at the address he had given her. Yes, she was free to meet that very afternoon if he wanted to.

That was how she found herself driving north from Meadowvale towards a terraced house in Leyton, wondering what Hargreaves wanted to share with her, racked with guilt for feeling a sliver of dread at the prospect of meeting him, another penniless and broken victim of the twenty-first century.

But the man who answered the door seemed sprightly and energetic, lean rather than skinny, his iron-grey hair and beard long but well-trimmed rather than unkempt. His eyes were the same metallic hue, and she searched them for a trace of the haunted, desperate look she associated with the capital's destitute; but the ashen orbs defied scrutiny, like lead shields. He was a tall man, but stooped as he spoke to her, making her feel as though she was being closely inspected.

'Thank you for coming,' he said. 'Follow me. I'll make you a cup of tea.'

'Where's your friend?' she asked as she followed him inside.

'Oh, don't worry, he says we can use the place all afternoon. He won't be back until later.'

He retained his stoop as he hurried off into the house, and she realised just how tall he was, so much so that he had to crouch under each doorway he passed through. She imagined him squashed behind the wheel of a taxi, folded away like some complex kitchen appliance.

She followed him along the short hallway, wondering if she

should take her shoes off but not seeing anywhere to leave them. Beneath her feet was a thick beige carpet that extended all the way up the staircase to her left, along which every available patch of wall space was covered with pictures of the homeowner's family. There was a small door below the stairs that presumably led into a broom cupboard, its corner sliced off to fit it into the cramped space. Hargreaves ducked through a larger door to the right, which led to the living room.

The beige carpet continued here, combining with the dark wallpaper and furnishings to make the space seem smaller than it was, adding to the already oppressive feel of the house. More photographs were scattered haphazardly across the walls as though blasted from a shotgun; some, their frames and sizes mismatched, sat on the shelf above the fireplace, which was occupied by an old-fashioned electric fire, the kind with fake coal inside it that glowed when you switched it on. The overall effect was like stepping through a time warp back into the 1970s.

'Do you take milk and sugar?' Hargreaves called from beyond another door. She could hear the sound of a kettle boiling and the tinkling of a teaspoon, and wondered whether the kitchen was as dated as the living room, with wood panelling on every cupboard and linoleum covering the floor.

'Just milk, please,' she replied, trying to figure out where to sit, in the end settling for the sagging navy-blue couch. She felt uncomfortable, possibly because she didn't quite understand why the owner of the house would be so keen for a homeless person to use it to entertain guests. She almost jumped when her phone vibrated in her pocket, then had to quickly compose herself as Hargreaves entered carrying two steaming mugs. He was wearing a plain black sweater and trousers that looked smarter, and cleaner, than she'd expected, and she silently berated herself for being so judgemental.

'So your friend lets you use his house? That's very kind of him.'

'Oh, not regularly. I don't take advantage, don't worry.' Hargreaves smiled and winked, although somehow the expression looked utterly out of place on his face. 'Just occasionally, as a special favour.'

'And you wanted to use it today to meet with me?'

'That's right,' Hargreaves said, taking a very deliberate slurp of his tea as though relishing every drop. 'It's great to finally meet you in person. I'm sorry I don't get much chance to listen to the show.'

'That's okay,' she replied, sipping her own drink. 'So what did you want to talk to me about?'

His gaze was fixed on her, and she felt again that she was being scrutinised. It was made all the more unsettling by the dead, grey hue of Hargreaves' eyes; like being stared at, really intently, by an inanimate object.

'First, I wanted to respond to your message,' he said. 'You were asking about my Facebook account.' Another long, noisy swig of tea punctuated his words, and she realised that another sound was bothering her: the ticking of the clock that she could see on the mantelpiece, partially hidden behind the photographs. It was one of those old-fashioned gold ones, the kind kept under a glass cover to prevent dust from damaging its internal mechanism. She happened to know that it was called a torsion clock, and that its incessant ticking was the sound of the swinging pendulum that enabled it to keep time fairly accurately, as long as it was wound up every few weeks.

'That's right. We've been receiving anonymous messages from someone calling themselves Lewis Carroll, and we managed to access their list of Facebook friends. Your name appeared in there.'

Hargreaves laughed, the sound oddly cold and mirthless.

The ticking in the background made her think of clockwork, of mechanical things impersonating human routines. 'Oh, yes, well. I bet you were surprised to find a homeless man with a Facebook account, eh?'

'Not necessarily. It's like your mobile phone – these things are part of modern life. I guess you can get internet access in the hostels, internet cafes and so on?'

He laughed again as though she'd said something funny, and took another glug of tea. The abrasive slurping sound almost put her off her own cup, but she continued to drink, conscious of not wanting to offend Hargreaves, feeling guilty for being so disconcerted by him.

'Part of modern life,' he said eventually, echoing her words. 'Like apps. Podcasts. Lots of new things for us all to get to grips with, eh?'

Her phone buzzed again, as if on cue.

'Do you mind if I just check my messages?' she asked. Hargreaves smiled and made a 'be my guest' gesture. She extracted the phone and saw a missed call from Isaac, along with a follow-up text.

Call me. We've heard from L.

Lukas Serafinowicz. Katrin's work colleague, who had been away travelling for months. Perhaps he'd be able to confirm some of the details from the night of the party.

'Do you need to make a call?' Hargreaves asked, as though reading her mind.

'I'll call them back in a while,' she said, smiling, determined to be polite. In the background, the clock ticked relentlessly, as though counting down the seconds before Hargreaves would be dumped back out onto the streets. 'So tell me, John – do you know anything about Lewis Carroll?'

JON RICHTER

'As a matter of fact, I do. That's really what I wanted to talk to you about.'

She raised an eyebrow. 'Go on.'

He leaned back in the armchair, seeming to stretch out fully for the first time, like an uncoiling spring. All the while his eyes remained fixed on hers, and she shifted her gaze to the mug of tea, which was pleasant if a little odd-tasting.

'Life is a strange thing,' he said cryptically. 'Sometimes it requires people to construct all sorts of different versions of themselves, just to get by. I don't just mean online; I mean in all aspects of our existence. Home, work, family, friends. Can you relate to that, Elaine?'

She nodded, confused. Keen to avoid his unfaltering stare, she found herself looking around the room, her gaze settling eventually on the photographs on the wall nearby. Something about them was nagging at her, a recurring detail that tugged insistently on a thread somewhere in her brain.

'Take me for example. When I was driving a taxi, I had to pretend to be oh-so happy to be doing it. As though the most important thing in my life was to serve others, to ferry them around gratefully, even if they insulted me or threw up in the back seat of my car.'

Something about his voice, or perhaps the rhythm of the clock, was making her feel sleepy. She squeezed her eyes closed and then open, trying to will the drowsiness out of them, focusing hard on the photographs while Hargreaves' bizarre monologue continued.

'And what about this Lewis Carroll? Clearly that person does not exist. But for whatever reason they have felt compelled to adopt this alternate personality. Like a mask, if you will – a mask they can wear to become somebody they aren't. At times they choose, of course. It's important that the process is under their control.'

Most of the pictures depicted a family, or a subset of the same individuals: a woman with four children.

'We all have masks, Elaine. It's perfectly normal. Healthy, even. Until someone decides to interfere, to try to forcibly *remove* a person's mask. I'm afraid that can cause all sorts of stress for everyone concerned.'

Her phone buzzed again, and she glanced absently at it, not bothering this time to ask Hargreaves' permission. Another message from Isaac. She frowned at it, feeling sure that what it said was important, but somehow unable to concentrate, to fully consider its implications.

Call me now. Jamal got the date wrong. The party was the week BEFORE Katrin disappeared.

'You're another good example,' Hargreaves' soporific drone continued. 'You wear a mask, when you record your podcast. Oh, yes, it's still Elaine Napier, the same name – but is it really the same person?'

Her eyes drifted to the mantelpiece, towards the clock, whose ticking was starting to feel like a hammer, pounding against her brain, beating her into unconsciousness like blows from a weapon.

'Or is the Elaine Napier that people tune in to listen to–'

'John,' she said, interrupting him. 'Did you put something in my tea?'

It was at that moment she noticed the picture adjacent to the clock. It wasn't a gradual realisation – instead, the understanding came in a jarring instant that seemed to blast the stupor from her mind. She rose almost before she even thought about it, dropping her half-finished cup to the floor, where it bounced but didn't shatter, splashing tea all over the carpet, beige on beige.

The photograph was a picture of a young man, wearing a suit and tie. It had clearly been taken a long time ago, but the likeness was unmistakable: it was Hargreaves, young and smiling into the camera, back when his hair had been brown and his eyes somehow not so monstrously empty.

'Damn,' he said simply as she moved towards the door. He rose effortlessly, seeming to snap into an upright position like an extendable weapon, a look of great regret crossing his face as he darted towards her. In a split second he had enfolded her in a tight embrace, his arms locked around her like a stick insect clinging determinedly to a tree branch. One of his hands had produced a hypodermic syringe from somewhere; the other clamped across her mouth as he slid the needle gently into the skin of her thigh.

'The tea might have worked, if you'd only waited longer,' he said reproachfully, in the tone you might use to scold a misbehaving puppy.

As she fell – only metaphorically, because Hargreaves' iron grip held her upright as she slid into oblivion – she could think only that the photograph on the mantelpiece was the same as Lewis Carroll's Facebook profile, and that the house had no kind-hearted, generous owner; it belonged to Hargreaves, and nobody else knew she was there.

49

THE LION, STEPNEY GREEN, 2008

'So when do I pay you?'

The lights in the pub were bright, but somehow the man sitting opposite her was still shrouded in shadow. His thin mouth was curled into a faintly mocking smile, and she couldn't help thinking how small it was, how all of his facial features looked just a little undersized, including his bald, domed head, as though it had simply stopped growing during his early adolescence. The effect was emphasised by his shoulders, which were alarmingly broad, giving the impression that he might burst out of his fag-ash-coloured suit at any moment.

'Very direct, aren't you?' he said in the same scouse-accented voice she'd heard on the phone. Its high pitch matched his head but not his body.

'It's my style.'

'Half now, and the other half when it's done.'

She nodded, relieved that he hadn't suddenly tried to jack up the price. She started to fumble in her bag, but he interrupted with a look of alarm.

'Don't pull it out in here,' he hissed. 'Leave it in the disabled toilet on your way out.'

She nodded again, her head spinning at how fast this whole thing was moving. It had only been a few days ago that her contact had mentioned the man who called himself Jimmy ('whatever you want, he'll fix it', as Frank had said), and now here she was, meeting him in person, about to hand over a wad of cash in a squalid East London dive.

Glancing around the pub, she wondered who he was worried about – every single punter was male, and each of them looked like he was more than well acquainted with witnessing brown envelopes changing hands. Those that weren't already slumped on the bar were staring at her, almost drooling with excitement at seeing a young blonde woman in their pub. Thankfully, her companion's presence seemed to be dissuading any of them from making an approach; whether because of his size or his reputation, she didn't know.

'How will you do it?'

He laughed at this, taking a sip of his lager. 'Better you don't know, love. I won't be doing it myself, though, that's for sure.'

'Oh.' Her face must have given away her disappointment, because he laughed again.

'Don't worry. It'll get done. I have a very reliable operative in there. It'll be next week, most probably Tuesday, although I can't guarantee the exact date. But I doubt that sack of shit will make the news, so you'll have to take my word for it.'

'Don't worry. I'll know when it's done. I'll feel it.'

He laughed again, taking another swig of his pint. Then he looked at her, his greenish eyes glistening like something toxic, his expression suddenly frighteningly serious. 'No. You won't. You're paying for revenge, but you won't get any satisfaction. Whatever he did, it'll still fucking haunt you. And once he's dead, so will he. To your grave.'

'Better that than let him live. He'll be out in a few months, with the rest of his life ahead of him.'

The bald man drained the rest of his glass. 'You're a cold woman, Elaine.'

She saw him again six days later.

50

'Good evening, Alice.'

The words seemed to come from inside her own brain, cutting through the swirling memories, a projection onto the canvas of baffling colours that confronted her as her eyes blinked themselves groggily open. The images swam and shifted, coalescing gradually into two main parts: the darkness of a dimly-lit room, and the pinkish-white of a face in its centre.

A face with lead-grey eyes, watching her.

'Alice, can you hear me?'

The same voice, but this time from outside her head, from the centre of the face that was the centre of the room. Someone speaking to her, cajoling her into wakefulness. She felt dust particles tickling her throat and coughed heavily, and with that sound and the convulsion of her body, she suddenly became aware of herself, of Elaine Napier, in a dark room, unable to move because her hands and feet were bound with heavy manacles that cut cruelly into her skin. She tugged against them in disbelief, feeling their weight as she sagged against the wall, kneeling as though in supplication before the face of her tormentor.

A face that sat at the top of a very long body, hinged at the waist as it stooped towards her, like an impossibly tall flower peering down to examine her.

'What the fuck did you inject me with?' she slurred.

'Better not to worry about the specifics,' said Hargreaves. 'It was the same sedative I used on Katrin, you'll be intrigued to learn.'

She opened her mouth, then closed it again as more possibilities exploded inside her brain.

The suitcase.

The party.

Jamal got the date wrong.

'But we tested it... there was no way you could do it in six minutes.'

'Yes, I've been enjoying listening to you try to puzzle it out. I've been lucky, I think, while you've been blundering off on wild goose chases. Some of which I'll admit were thanks to me. Or should I say, thanks to your friend Lewis Carroll.'

A grin split his face, but still those lead-grey eyes were bereft of humour, as devoid of warmth as two chunks of scrap metal.

The floor beneath her was cold, too. No thick carpet here, wherever they were: just flat, featureless concrete on all sides, illuminated by a dim lightbulb hanging above them.

'It was you who sent us the footage... you told the building manager you were a policeman.'

'An old Ted Bundy trick, that one. The thing is, even when people ask to see your ID, you can just show them any old rubbish. They don't know what a real police warrant card looks like.'

A basement, perhaps, beyond that door under the stairs. She tried to imagine Hargreaves bending to pass through it, and the image was so peculiar she almost laughed.

'You were trying to distract us. You were worried we'd solve the case.'

'If everybody minded their own business, the world would go round a deal faster than it does,' he said, smile still hanging there like something nailed in place.

'What did you do to her?' she said, trying to keep him talking while she strained at her bonds. The shackles at her wrists and ankles felt rock-solid, as though the stone of the wall and floor had grown around her while she slept. 'Did you bring her here, too?'

'The first stage of a long process. I remember her being defiant too, in the beginning.'

Napier's eyes began to adjust to the gloom, and panic rose in her chest as she made out other shapes: a crude wooden bed, a metal bucket, a single door that hinged outwards, thick and sturdy.

'How... long was she down here for?'

It was then that she finally realised what she was wearing. Gone was her shapeless grey sweater, her comfortable jeans, her battered trainers. Instead she was wearing a powder-blue dress that stretched to just beyond her knees, covered with a white pinafore.

'She lasted nearly three years in the end. She killed herself, like they always do. I try to leave nothing to chance, but somehow they find a way. In her case it was edge of the bed frame – she managed to scrape it sharp enough to slash her wrists on it.' He said this in the tone with which you might mourn the passing of a pet hamster, or a pot plant that you overwatered by mistake.

'How many have there been?' Napier asked, trying to keep the horror out of her voice while she racked her brain for a solution, an opportunity, any means by which she might avoid that door closing, sealing her down here in this concrete prison.

To become the plaything of a monster.

'You'll be number seven. It has a nice ring to it, doesn't it? Lucky seven. A prime number.'

'People know I'm here, John,' she lied. 'My friends, my colleagues. Everyone will suspect something when the show suddenly goes off the air.'

'Yes, yes, there will be an investigation, an outcry, some kerfuffle or other. But it will die down. They always do.' Another soulless smile carved itself across his face. 'And if anyone does come here, they'll just find poor old John Hargreaves, the retired Ryde driver, clinging to the memory of his wife and children.'

Her face fell as another realisation sank like a dropped anchor into her brain. 'You never had a wife and kids, did you?'

He shook his head patiently. 'One of my masks. As I was trying to explain earlier, before you decided to make a scene.'

'I'll shout. I'll scream. Someone will hear me,' she said desperately.

'Soundproof walls. I installed them myself. You could yell yourself hoarse down here and no one would have a clue.'

'If you come near me, I'll bite your fucking cock off,' she hissed.

'I've heard it all before, Alice. A few days without food usually does the trick.'

'Stop calling me that, you fucking sicko!' She tugged desperately against the chains, but they were as unyielding as before, as unyielding as they'd been for years, for the six other women who had died down here before her.

For the six other Alices.

For Katrin.

Hargreaves, or whoever he was, took a step backwards, still watching her, his expression tinged with wistfulness. 'You know, I had no interest in you at all, except as another investigator, another detective I needed to outwit. But then I looked you up online. You really are a very pretty girl, underneath all the jaded cynicism.' He moved closer to the door, inserting himself into the gap where a staircase led upwards and out, back to where the world was marginally less insane. 'A bit old for my tastes, but you know what they say: beggars can't be choosers.'

He smiled one last time, a terrible smile like a robotic approximation, as though he'd learned it from pictures. 'Goodnight, Alice,' he said. Then he stepped outside, and began to close the door. Napier concentrated hard on clamping shut her mouth, not wanting to give him the satisfaction of a despairing scream as she was consigned to darkness.

Then there was a loud crack, and the monster that called itself John Hargreaves crumpled back into the room, collapsing like a Jenga tower. She stared, bewildered, into the gap between the door and its frame. Microseconds passed like hours, as though time itself had frozen, a pendulum caught at its apex.

Then Wim Hellendoorn stepped into view, wearing his Columbo coat and battered fedora, wielding his cane like a club. Their eyes met, and for a moment he was the most incredible sight she had ever seen. Relief escaped from her in a huge, elated, euphoric sigh.

'Nice dress,' he said eventually.

'Just get me out of here before he wakes up,' she snapped, unable to keep the smile from her face. 'How did you even find me?'

'Isaac told me about the call from Serafinowicz,' Hellendoorn replied as he rummaged in the pockets of the man he'd just laid out. 'The party wasn't on the thirty-first. It was the week before, on the twenty-fourth. Your whole investigation was on the wrong track from the start. It didn't help that Hargreaves fucked with the date stamp on the CCTV footage. Oh sod it,' he added, giving up his search. 'These will have to do.' He brandished his trusty set of skeleton keys like a proud gaoler.

'Shit. I can't believe it. We were completely wrong.' She thought about what it meant, about the party and Weaver and the box full of teeth, but it felt like too much to hold inside her head all at once. 'But how did that lead you here?'

'I knew Hargreaves was connected to Lewis Carroll, online. And I knew it was strange for you not to get in touch after the text messages. So I just started trying a few options. This is the same place where I met him, years ago. The same photos on the walls. They're bullshit, aren't they? His wife and kids?'

'Utter,' she replied as he unlocked the chains. She winced as she rubbed at her wrists; after even a few hours the restraints had scraped the joints raw. She didn't want to think about the condition that Katrin had been in by the time she decided to end her life, the damage that years trapped in a room like this could do to a person.

'So... this is where Katrin died?' the detective asked in a hollow, melancholy voice.

Napier nodded sadly.

'Did he tell you how he did it?' Hellendoorn asked. 'How he managed to beat the six minutes?'

'No,' she replied, rising woozily to her feet. 'But maybe he'll explain it to the police, when they interrogate him.'

'Or maybe he won't,' growled Hellendoorn, something dangerous glinting in his eyes. 'Maybe he'll just clam up forever, or commit suicide in his cell.'

'What are you saying?'

Hellendoorn bent, scooping Hargreaves under the armpits, and began to drag the tall man's prone body backwards towards the manacles. Napier watched, perplexed, then gasped as she realised what her friend intended to do.

'You can't, Wim. It's too much. There are boundaries.'

'It's been too long, Elaine,' he said, as he began to attach the chains to Hargreaves' wrists. 'In case you haven't noticed, I haven't got much to live for.' He struggled to haul Hargreaves into a sitting position, then stopped, turning to look at her. His eyes glistened wetly as he spoke.

'I just need to know what happened.'

She watched as he set about fastening the shackles around the killer's ankles. She thought about everything that man had done, his life of lies and atrocities. The horror he had wrought upon Gunnar and Anna, two kind and simple people who had just wanted to show their daughter the very best of the world.

She thought about Sam, a teenage girl whose life was snuffed out by a man exactly like that. A creature of lust and need and self. A monster beyond rehabilitation. A predator.

She thought about that night, 31 January 2013, when somehow Hargreaves had transported Katrin's suitcase upstairs, then made her disappear, all in a sliver of time no longer than a morning shower.

'So do I,' she said, as she bent to help him.

51

SPECIAL BROADCAST:

THE TRUTH

To search for the truth is a strange goal. Perhaps if we had an infinite amount of time, we could mash more and more information into our brains, gradually absorbing the entirety of the world's data like a supercomputer. But we don't have an infinite time; far from it, in fact. We have such a pitiful sliver of time that we are forced to specialise; to select specific truths, those we want to pursue, to invest our life's energy in. We immerse ourselves in these truths until they come to define us.

For some this is history, painstakingly unearthing the truth of our planet's past in the form of fossils and medieval texts, or the ruins of ancient buildings, or monarchs buried in car parks. Others look to the future, seeking the truth of science to cure diseases or to explain the universe, to enable us to explore further into its vast expanse. For many, the truth of love and family is enough, the unbreakable bonds they've formed with their parents and siblings and children, the axles upon which human life revolves.

This case became my truth. I was fixated, obsessed even, with learning what happened to Katrin Gunnarsdottir on that cold January night, exactly six years ago at the time of recording. But I've learned that when you pursue one truth, sometimes you uncover many others, quite by accident.

Let's start with Tony Weaver. Here is a man who may be involved in countless unsolved crimes, a violent thug who takes his victim's teeth as trophies, even wearing some around his neck. Katrin attended a party at his apartment, where he made advances on her. But the party didn't happen on the night of her disappearance. This we learned from Lukas Serafinowicz, who accompanied her that night. Thank you, Lukas, for your help. Jamal Habib, no hard feelings – you just misremembered the date. It turns out you gave up your Dry January vow a week earlier than you thought, and none of the people we interviewed remembered the party well enough to correct our wrong assumption. The building manager would have known, of course, because he'd have known the real date of the CCTV footage – but I never thought to double-check it. It's no wonder the police never took the party seriously as a lead. I can see, now, the extent of my failure; how our entire investigation was built upon this flawed foundation.

It was doomed from the start.

No, Katrin returned home from that party safe and sound, and never told her boyfriend about it. It was a week later when she caught a Ryde home after her brief visit to Iceland. And now, finally, we know the truth of where she went.

Her body will be discovered, after this episode is released, buried in the back garden of 442 Garrett Lane. I'm sure the podcast will quickly be taken down, but not before enough people have listened to know that her bones are interred with those of five other women, each smashed into small pieces and buried inside a separate, large metal waste bin. The other women's names are Sally Sparkes, Moira Davies, Marta Novotny,

Tilly Henderson, and Sarah Jaques. Like me, they all had blonde hair, the type that a man calling himself John Hargreaves prefers.

You remember John; he was the driver of the Ryde that Katrin took home on the night of her disappearance.

<Cracking sound, followed by spluttering and moaning>

That's John. He told Katrin his car boot wasn't working, so her suitcase would have to go on the back seat with her in the front. This enabled him to inject her with a fast-acting sedative while the car was in motion, rendering her unconscious by the time they arrived at her address. He then spent six minutes stuffing her into the vehicle's ample boot, along with her suitcase, before calmly continuing with his rounds. Hours later, he dropped off the suitcase at her address, before driving the still-comatose Katrin to Garrett Lane, where he lives.

That's where we're recording right now, in the dungeon beneath his house, where he kept his victims until they died. He built it all by himself, accessible through the cupboard under the stairs: a soundproof concrete cube, complete with a bed and bucket and manacles. This is where he starved the poor women into submission, making them dress like Alice from Lewis Carroll's stories, acting out his perverted fantasies.

Isn't that right, John?

<Another crack and a muffled cry, then coughing and spitting sounds>

Yes, it turns out John has an obsession with Lewis Carroll, for reasons he is unable or unwilling to articulate. He used to make the girls wear a little blue dress, and call them Alice, until they became so sick of living as his prisoners that they killed themselves. He even called himself Lewis Carroll online, the alias under which he messaged us several times, desperately trying to steer our investigation off track.

And now that investigation is over, and I'm learning another thing about the pursuit of truth: sometimes, that pursuit can come at a cost. Look at the damage we've done to date.

Let's start with Blake Horowitz, the former project director of Hannibal Heights, the apartment building that replaced the taxidermy museum in Meadowvale. Katrin's boss, in a manner of speaking, or at least a senior executive to whom she was subordinate in Triton Homes' complex matrix organisation. He may or may not have had an affair with Katrin, but it's certainly true that he had several extra-marital interludes, ultimately resulting in the end of his marriage. Horowitz threatened me, personally, after he was mentioned on this podcast, with both legal recourse and physical violence.

I learned a couple of days ago that Horowitz was found dead at his home in Clapham, a suspected suicide via a drug overdose. He may have been an unpleasant man, and a cheat, but did he really deserve to die like that?

He can be added to the toll of Marcus Dobson, who is in jail and awaiting trial for attacking an innocent man. That innocent man was Michael Fairclough, who has emerged from his coma, but is still recovering in hospital from his injuries. Meanwhile, Michael's poor mother, who was dependent upon him for her care, is being looked after by social workers, while her back garden has been demolished in a fruitless search for evidence linking her son to John's crimes.

And what about Martina Mazziotto; did she deserve to be publicly accused on this very podcast, before her name was cleared?

That's another thing about the quest for truth. When you finally find it, and look back at the trail of carnage in your wake, you find yourself asking... was it worth it?

Well, John, I've decided to absolve myself completely of that responsibility. It's just too much for me to bear. Which means there are five crimes, plus six murders, for which you'll have to suffer the consequences. That's eleven sentences altogether, back to back.

And I'm going to make sure they're very severe, John. In fact, I'm going to throw the book at you.

<Sound of indistinct mumbling>

Before we finish the interview, I'd just like to say thank you to my colleague, Isaac Jones, whose tireless efforts have made all this possible. He is not in any way involved in this final episode, nor does he condone or approve of my actions. Please, Isaac, just know that I had to do this, and that once I'd decided there was nothing you could have done to stop me.

You know how stubborn I am.

I'd also like to dedicate this podcast to my sister, Sam. She was killed 26 years ago by someone just like John. His name was Eric Batson, and he died in jail – and that was *my* crime. I can't lay that one at your doorstep, John. I paid someone to do him in, and they delivered, and he was brutally stabbed to death in the prison changing rooms. This final episode, therefore, is my confession. I'm happy to elaborate further after my arrest. I just want to be honest, completely honest, with everyone.

Including you, John. So I need to tell you this is going to hurt, a great deal. And while we're going through this process, I want you to think hard about all the things you've done to women, over the years. All the times you've turned the key in a lock to imprison them. All the times you've heaved that thick door closed, sealing them inside. All the times you've prepared a syringe to take with you while collecting taxi fares, just in case an irresistible blonde happened to climb into your front seat.

All the times you've looked at a woman and thought, *There's another easy victim.*

These are things you won't be able to do, ever again.

<Muffled> 'No, no, please, I told you, I told you everything... you said you'd let me go!'

<Sound of indistinct whimpering and begging, then a scream, followed by a series of cracking sounds. The screams gradually fade to sobbing, then to a bubbling gargle, and finally to silence.>

EPILOGUE

It was early March, and a small group was gathered outside Lagafellskirkja, the closest church to Mosfellsbaer. The weather was fairly average for the locals, or bitterly cold if you were a foreigner, as two of the congregation were, and the air carried a sprinkling of fine powdery snow. Some of these fragments settled on the coffin, lost immediately against its brilliant white surface. Others were caught in the hair of the choir members, who would sing traditional songs after the priest had finished his reading. Everything was in Icelandic, of course, meaning the foreigners couldn't understand the words.

Embalming is not commonplace in Iceland, so funerals usually happen just days after death, but in this case the deceased had been dead for a long time, meaning that Gunnar and Anna had had time to arrange something more elaborate than this simple ceremony. But they hadn't wanted to; they desired simply to remember their beloved daughter, and to say goodbye. The casket was far too large for the scant fragments that remained of Katrin's body, but its dimensions suggested a human form inside, because that was the form that they wished to recollect, and to mourn. The form of a girl who had been beautiful – 'on the outside, on the inside, everywhere', as someone had once said.

The choir started, their voices drowning out the hum of the wind, and Isaac felt a tear rolling down his cheek, and wondered whether it would freeze there before it fell. He thought about a lot of things while they sang: he thought about death and life, about winter and spring, about closure and new beginnings.

He thought about Michael Fairclough, and the garden that he had helped 'the Coughing Man' to rebuild.

He thought about Wim Hellendoorn, and the sentence that awaited him for assisting in a murder. Given the detective's age and health, he was likely to die in jail.

He thought about Elaine, and the quest for truth that had destroyed her, and wondered when he would be able to visit her in prison.

He thought about Martina Mazziotto, who stood beside him, around a foot shorter in height but powerful, both physically and in spirit. He saw tears in her eyes too, and without thinking too much about it, he reached out a hand. She held it, and squeezed, and together they watched as the frozen dust continued to swirl.

ACKNOWLEDGMENTS

I would like to give a huge thank you to Betsy, Fred and everyone else at Bloodhound Books for their help and support in bringing another one of my weird stories to life. Particular thanks go to Clare for her invaluable assistance during the editing process – there were a lot of dates and timings to check!

Without the support of my family and friends there is no way I would ever write anything, so I want to give enormous thanks to everyone who read or contributed to various drafts of this, particularly to Shuo for putting up with my constant enthusiastic waffling about it, my uncle Russell for taking the time to read and give detailed and immensely useful feedback on a nearly-final version, and my mum for coming up with a much better title than my original (rubbish) one!

Printed in Great Britain
by Amazon